BENEAT.. ..._ _

ISBN 9798282858266

© 2025 Ulf Brånebro

Email: ulf.branebro@quillstonepress.com

Instagram: @ulfbranebro

Facebook: @ulf.branebro

Quillstone Press

https://www.quillstonepress.com/

BENEATH THE LID

Ulf Brånebro

THE ONES WHO GET CHOSEN

The first book in the series

Thank you for reading **Beneath the Lid**. This story stands on its own. You don't have to read anything else first.

However, for the best reading experience and to better understand Patrik and the village of Keldarp — and the silences that echo through it — you might want to begin with **The Ones Who Get Chosen**.

It's the first in the series. A quiet book about a brutal crime, and the people who carry its weight.

It's also quite short, so you'll be able to get back to this one in no-time. **Scan the QR code** to get your copy.

PROLOGUE

Beneath the Lid

She woke to nothing.

No light. No sound. Just the weight of her own breathing — too fast, too loud.

The air pressed against her skin, warm and stale, carrying the faint scent of varnished wood and something sour — sweat, maybe fear.

Her heart was already racing before her mind caught up. The kind of panic that came from routine, not danger.

The kids.

She tried to sit up. Her forehead hit something hard. Confusion sharpened into urgency.

Her hands moved instinctively, reaching out, but they found walls where there shouldn't be any. Smooth. Close. Too close.

Her chest tightened — not from lack of air, not yet — but from the simple, brutal thought that she was late. Again.

Daycare would be closing. They'd be waiting by the window, small faces scanning every car that wasn't hers. The nannies would be judging her. As they always do.

Her hand fumbled down her side, searching for the phone. The lifeline. Fingers closed around it with a tremble she didn't notice yet.

She lifted the phone as far as the space allowed, angling it in tight circles. No signal — *Searching...*

Two missed calls. Three messages. Daycare

"Just checking if you're on your way? We're closing soon."

"We really need to lock up. Please let us know."

"Unable to reach you. Proceeding according to protocol."

Her thumb hovered, useless. No signal. No connection. The world above might as well have been on another planet.

Her breath caught in her throat. She opened the settings, switched on the flashlight.

The beam cut through the dark — revealing smooth, pale wood inches from her face. The grain was fresh, clean. It smelled like pine, sharp and new, mixed with something else. Soil.

Her eyes followed the narrow space — walls too close, too neat. The bedding beneath her was crisp, white, tucked in like a display. Decorative stitching along the edges. A pillow under her head, soft but hollow in meaning.

The shape of it all settled in her mind before the word did.

Having worked at the Coffin factory for years, she immediately recognized the model. Björkö, named after a quiet island on the west coast of Sweden. Solid pine. One of their best sellers.

The light flickered — once, then again. She tapped the phone, but it was already fading.

When the screen went black, it wasn't sudden. It was slow. Like the phone knew it was the last thing she'd ever see, and didn't want to leave her too quickly.

Then nothing. Just dark. And the sound of her own breathing, growing sharper by the second.

The dark felt heavier now. Thicker.

Her hands moved before thought could catch up — palms flat against the surface above her, pushing hard enough to make her shoulders burn.

Nothing gave.

She pushed again, harder this time. The smooth surface stayed firm, unmoved, like it had been waiting for this moment.

Her breath came fast — too fast. Each inhale sharper, each exhale louder. The space filled with the sound of her own panic.

Fingers curled into fists. She slammed them against the wood. Once. Twice. A third time — until pain shot up her arms and blurred into something else.

She didn't stop.

Nails scraped at the edges, searching for seams that weren't there. The tips splintered first, then tore. Warmth spread across her fingertips — sticky, unseen.

The scream came without warning. Raw. Useless. It bounced back at her, swallowed by the walls that pressed closer with every second.

Her throat burned, but she screamed again — a sound that didn't belong to words, just fear too big to hold inside.

Her chest heaved. The air already felt thinner, warmer. Each breath tasted of wood and sweat and something metallic.

She kept clawing, kept hitting, because stopping meant accepting. And she wasn't ready for that. Not yet.

But her arms were getting heavy. The punches weaker. The scrapes slower.

The screams faded into nothing.

Her throat was raw, breath shallow — more gasps than air now. Words came without thinking, shaky and quiet.

"Please…"

No one answered. She didn't expect them to.

The words shifted, old and half-forgotten, but they came anyway. A rhythm from childhood. Something to hold onto.

Our Father, who art in heaven,
hallowed be Thy name.
Thy kingdom come,
Thy will be done,
on earth as it is in heaven.
Give us this day our daily bread,
and forgive us our trespasses,
as we forgive those who trespass against us.
And lead us not into temptation,
but deliver us from evil.
For thine is the kingdom,
the power and the glory,
forever and ever.
Amen.

She whispered it again. And again. Not for salvation — just because silence was worse.

Somewhere between the lines, their faces appeared. Two small girls, hair tangled from sleep, giggling over pancakes. Sticky fingers, blueberry jam on their cheeks.

They were safe now. Far from his shouting. Far from his bottles and his anger.

She let the words carry her, not because she believed — but because there was nothing else left to say. Nothing else to hope for.

The words ran out before the air did.

Her lips moved, but no sound followed. Even the prayer had abandoned her now.

Each breath came thinner. Shallow pulls of warmth that tasted wrong — like breathing through a blanket pressed too tight.

Her arms felt distant, too heavy to lift. Fingers slack against the blood-slick wood.

The pounding in her chest slowed. Not calm — just tired.

Thoughts drifted, untethered. A shoe left in the hallway. A half-finished shopping list on the fridge. The sound of laughter she couldn't quite place anymore.

There was no fear left. Only the dull weight of everything slipping away.

The edges of herself blurred. Breathing became something she noticed, then forgot.

Silence settled in — not around her, but inside.

And then there was nothing.

CHAPTER 1

A Village Morning

The door clicked open without ceremony. Aram, who owned Pizzeria Napoli together with his brother Dilan slid the key from the lock, pushed the handle down, and let the morning air follow him inside. It smelled like it always did — yesterday's fry oil, coffee grounds gone stale, and something faintly sweet from the candy shelf. He didn't turn on the lights. The pale summer sun did enough through the fogged windows.

Patrik was already there. Or maybe it just felt that way. He'd slipped in behind Aram, a nod exchanged that barely registered. No words. Just routine.

He took his usual seat by the window, where condensation blurred the view of Road 46. The world outside moved, but in here it stayed the same. A laminated menu stuck to his elbow when he shifted. He didn't bother peeling it off. The table was always like that — wiped, but never clean.

The TV on the wall flickered to life, sound muted. Some morning news anchor gesturing at headlines no one in Keldarp cared about. Patrik watched without watching. His coffee arrived without being ordered. Aram placed it down with a glance, nothing more.

The first sip tasted like metal and burnt filters. Patrik didn't react. Across the room, Aram counted coins from the till, the soft clink of coins against cheap plastic breaking the quiet.

Outside, a car passed. Or maybe a truck. The window didn't offer details — just shapes moving through mist and glass smeared by years of indifferent cleaning.

Patrik let his gaze rest there. Not looking at anything in particular. Just sitting in the weight of a morning that felt like every other — except for the part that didn't.

The door chimed, a dull sound against the low hum of the fridge. Two men shuffled in — the kind who didn't need to order because Aram already knew. They didn't greet Patrik. Just a glance, then straight to the counter where the coffee pot sat waiting.

Patrik didn't turn his head. He heard them — the scrape of stools, the hiss of poured coffee, the first sip taken with a satisfied grunt. Silence lingered until habit broke it.

"Late again," one of them said. Not loud, but enough.

The other gave a short breath through his nose — almost a laugh, almost agreement.

"Can't count on some folks," he added, the words heavy with something that wasn't concern.

Patrik kept his eyes on the TV. The news had moved to weather — sunshine along the coast, rain further north. None of it mattered here.

Behind him, the conversation stayed low. No names. No need. Everyone knew who 'she' was. The rhythm of gossip didn't require introductions.

"Kids'll suffer, that's for sure," the first voice muttered, the scrape of a spoon against a ceramic cup marking the end of the sentence.

Aram wiped the counter in slow circles. His face gave nothing away. Just another morning, another story passing through the steam of cheap coffee.

Patrik shifted slightly, the laminated menu pulling at his sleeve again. Outside, the condensation on the window had begun to clear at the edges, revealing the empty street beyond.

The voices behind him faded into the clink of cups and the rustle of a newspaper being unfolded. No urgency. No alarm. Just two men filling the quiet with words that sounded like care, but weren't.

The door closed again, softer this time. A faint waft of perfume cut through the fry oil and coffee — something floral, out of place here. Patrik didn't need to look. He recognized the measured footsteps, the deliberate pause by the counter.

Cecilia Lövgren carried herself like she belonged — not just in the room, but in the structure of things. Church warden. Lövgren by blood. Keeper of minutes, memory, and manners. Her medium brown hair was gathered into a loose bun streaked with silver, glasses perched just low enough to glance over when needed. Conservative coat. No makeup. She moved like a woman used to quiet compliance.

Aram poured her coffee without being asked. She accepted it with a nod, settling into a chair near the counter. Not at Patrik's table. Not too far either. Just close enough.

She stirred her cup without adding anything. Just motion — circular, thoughtful, slow.

"It's good to see responsibility still matters," she said, her voice low but clear enough to carry. The words floated in the stale air, landing where they were meant to.

The regulars gave small noises of agreement — not words, just the comfortable murmur of shared opinion.

"Andreas… doing what's needed. Some men don't run from duty."

No one corrected her. The court order stayed unspoken. So did everything else.

She set the spoon aside. Adjusted the cup so it aligned with the edge of the saucer. Her fingers lingered a second longer than necessary.

Patrik didn't look at her. He watched her reflection shift in the window — a blur of posture, stillness, and control. Outside, the mist had cleared. Inside, nothing had.

The spoon came to rest. Silence followed — not awkward, just the kind that settled when everything that needed saying had been said.

Patrik's coffee had cooled. He didn't drink from it again. His gaze drifted to the window, where the last of the condensation clung to the corners. His reflection met him there — faint, distorted. Lines around his eyes sharper in the dull light.

Behind him, chairs scraped as one of the regulars shifted his weight. The newspaper rustled. Cecilia's cup touched the saucer with a soft click. Routine sounds, familiar enough to be ignored by anyone who wanted to.

Patrik didn't turn around. He watched the street appear through the glass — the cracked pavement, the leaning signpost by the bus stop. Nothing moved out there now. The village had already settled into its day.

His hand rested on the table, fingers tracing the edge of the sticky menu without thought. The laminated surface tugged slightly with each movement, anchoring him in place.

No one spoke to him. No one expected him to join in. That was how it worked here — silence wasn't absence. It was participation of a different kind.

He let the quiet stretch, feeling the weight of what hadn't been said pressing heavier than any words could manage.

In the window, his reflection blurred again as a cloud passed over the sun. It didn't stay long. Light returned — but the heaviness didn't lift.

The rumble came before the sight — low and uneven, a familiar stutter of an EPA tractor pushing down Road 46. Patrik's eyes shifted to the window as its reflection smeared across the glass. Faded paint, a crooked antenna, and a too-loud speaker rattling bass that couldn't be heard from inside. It passed without urgency, swallowed by the village beyond.

Behind him, chairs scraped back. The regulars rose, cups left half-finished, coins placed beside them without counting. A grunt served as farewell. The door swung open, then closed, the bell above it giving a half-hearted chime.

Cecilia stayed a moment longer, smoothing her skirt as she stood. Her gaze drifted across the room but never landed on Patrik. She adjusted her bag on her shoulder with both hands — a gesture of finality — then walked out without a word. The bell marked her exit, sharper this time.

Aram moved from behind the counter, cloth in hand, wiping down where no new customers waited. His movements were steady, practiced — clearing away what little trace remained of the morning's conversation.

Patrik watched the condensation finally vanish from the window, leaving only clear glass and the dull view of an empty street. He pushed his cup slightly forward. Aram didn't need to ask if he wanted a refill. He didn't.

The TV kept flickering in the corner, headlines shifting to something foreign and distant. Outside, the hum of the village settled back into its usual rhythm — nothing pressing, nothing wrong. Just another day.

Patrik stayed seated, letting the weight of knowing sit with him. No one else would carry it. Not here.

CHAPTER 2

A Missing Mother

The phone vibrated against the worn wood of the kitchen table. A low, insistent hum that didn't belong.

Patrik glanced at the screen without reaching for it. The coffin factory's number. He let it buzz a moment longer before picking up.

"Bockgren."

"Hi, yes — sorry to bother you on your private number." The voice was light, almost cheerful. A woman. "It's Lena from HR at the factory."

He stayed silent, waiting.

"It's just... well, Sofia Karlsson-Lindqvist hasn't shown up this week." A pause, the sound of papers shuffling. "Not that it's a big deal. These things happen."

Patrik looked at the coffee cup by his hand. The ring it had left on the table was already drying.

"And?"

"Oh, nothing official," she rushed. "It's just... you know how small places are. Thought maybe you could check in? Off the record, of course." A nervous laugh followed — the kind people used when asking for favors they didn't want to owe.

He could hear the hum of fluorescent lights in the background. The faint clatter of keyboards. Life going on.

"When did she last call in?"

"Well…" Another shuffle. "She didn't. But Sofia's… independent. Sometimes a bit, you know…She's our best sales rep, no doubt about it. And she gets along great with her accounts. She fits in much better at the conventions than she does here. In Keldarp. At the factory. She doesn't play by the rules." The sentence trailed off, left to hang where judgments lived.

Patrik let the silence answer for him.

"Anyway," Lena filled the gap, "if you're in the area… it'd just put minds at ease."

The call ended with polite thanks and a promise he never gave. The phone screen dimmed, leaving only the reflection of the window behind him — clear skies, nothing unusual.

Patrik finished his coffee. The cup was cold.

The morning light dulled behind dusty windows. Inside, the factory smelled of sawdust and varnish — familiar, heavy. Machines hummed in the distance, steady as a heartbeat no one noticed anymore.

The office was small and in need of a renovation.

Patrik walked past rows of desks, their wooden surfaces smudged with years of hands that came and went. One desk stood out only because it didn't — untouched, uncluttered, indifferent. A faded photo in a frame next to the monitor. Two girls, one holding the other's hand, both squinting into sunlight that didn't reach here. He picked it up.

"She's always been a bit... unpredictable." Lena's voice drifted from behind him. Apologetic, but bored. "These types, you know how it is."

Patrik didn't answer. His eyes stayed on the photo. The younger girl's shoes were on the wrong feet. No one had fixed it before the picture was taken.

Lena shifted her weight, heels clicking softly against the wooden floor. "She's had... episodes before. Not like this, but she runs her own race. We try to be understanding. After all, the results matter."

The fluorescent light above them flickered once. Neither of them looked up.

"Her bag's still here," Lena offered, as if that explained everything and nothing at once.

Patrik returned the photo frame with a dull clang. The sound barely rose above the machinery's hum.

"If she turns up, tell her payroll needs her hours," Lena added, already stepping away. "Otherwise, we'll have to adjust."

He watched her disappear down the corridor — clipboard in hand, duty done.

Outside, the air carried the faint scent of varnish and machine oil, trailing from the open loading bay. The factory doors closed behind Patrik with a hollow thud — the kind that didn't echo, just ended.

He stood still for a moment, boots on gravel, the hum of machinery seeping through concrete walls. A forklift beeped somewhere out of sight. Voices murmured in the distance, indistinct and uninterested.

The sky was clear. Too bright for the feeling in his chest.

Patrik adjusted his jacket, not because he was cold, but because there was nothing else to do with his hands. He looked back once — a row of windows, dusty and blank. No one watched. No one needed to.

The rhythm of the place didn't falter. Wood shavings drifted near the loading dock, catching on the wind before settling back into place. Routine swallowing concern — like it always did.

He walked towards his car, each step grinding against loose stones. The factory's hum faded with distance, but it never really disappeared. It lingered — the sound of work continuing, as if absence didn't matter.

At the driver's door, he paused. Glanced at the building one last time. Couldn't shake off the photo of the girls.

He got in. Started the engine. The dashboard clock blinked a time that felt too early to feel this heavy.

He drove back to Ulricehamn. Logged the visit. Filled in the fields. No one asked why.

By the time the afternoon round was done and Sebbe slid into the passenger seat for evening patrol, the sky had already turned the color of ash.

The tires crunched over gravel as they rolled out. Behind them, the day kept moving — quietly, like it always did.

That same evening, the beam of headlights cut through the mist curling over the empty road. Fields stretched out on either side, fading into grey. The radio crackled now and then — nothing urgent, nothing for them.

Patrik kept one hand on the wheel, the other resting near the gearstick. Sebbe sat beside him, legs stretched, fingers drumming lightly against his thigh in some rhythm only he knew.

"By the way," Patrik said, eyes on the road. "That woman I mentioned. Sofia. Still gone. Few days now."

Sebbe glanced over, a faint smirk pulling at his mouth. "Yeah? She probably needed a break. Can't blame her."

The mist thickened ahead, swallowing the outlines of the next bend. Sebbe leaned back, adjusting his vest like it mattered out here.

"Taking care of the girls after the divorce can't exactly be a holiday," he added, half-laughing. "Doesn't excuse her just taking off and dumping them on Andreas like that..."

Patrik didn't respond. The wipers squeaked once across a dry windshield before he switched them off. The road narrowed, gravel whispering under the tires now.

Sebbe shifted in his seat, pulling out his phone, thumb scrolling through nothing important. "It's always the same with these things. People get dramatic, then come back like nothing happened."

The patrol car rolled on, engine humming steady. The mist pressed closer, softening the edges of the world outside.

Patrik's eyes stayed forward. He didn't correct him.

The car slowed as the mist thickened, swallowing the last of the daylight. Headlights stretched only a few meters now, the beams fading into pale nothing.

Patrik eased off the accelerator. The road was just a suggestion beneath the tires — gravel muted by damp air.

Sebbe had gone quiet, his phone dim in his hand. The kind of silence that didn't need filling.

Patrik's gaze drifted to the fields beyond the ditch. Where crops should have been, there was only grey. The mist lay heavy over the land, smoothing out every shape, hiding what was always there.

He pulled the car over without a word. Let the engine idle, then switched off the lights. Darkness pressed in, soft but absolute.

For a long moment, neither of them moved. The faint tick of cooling metal the only sound between them.

Patrik opened the door and stepped out. The air was colder here — wet against his skin. He stood by the roadside, watching the way the mist curled and shifted, as if something beneath it was breathing slow and deep.

Somewhere out there, a farmhouse light flickered, then disappeared again.

Behind him, Sebbe stayed in the car. No questions asked.

Patrik didn't know what he was expecting to see. He only knew that the village wasn't looking — and whatever was coming had already arrived.

Rumors had it that the divorce hadn't been easy. Other rumors that Andreas hadn't only beat Sofia, but the girls as well. Patrik wasn't the one to listen to rumors, but court orders limiting a parent from spending time with his children alone didn't come out of nowhere.

The mist settled around him. Quiet. Patient.

He stayed until the weight in his chest felt like part of the landscape.

CHAPTER 3

The Husband's Calm

The lasagna was still warm when Patrik stepped out of the car. He balanced it with one hand, the foil tray sagging slightly in the middle. The plastic bag crinkled faintly in the quiet — no wind, no traffic. Just the late afternoon light settling over the gravel driveway like dust. The house looked clean from the outside. Curtains drawn, hedges clipped. The kind of order that asked not to be disturbed.

He wore jeans, a navy windbreaker zipped halfway up, sneakers with scuffed soles. No badge. No notebook. Just a caring neighbor with dinner in his hands, standing where no one had asked him to come. He paused at the base of the front steps. A bird chirped once from the lilac bush and then thought better of it. Somewhere behind the facade, a child's voice rose, then fell — not quite laughter. Then silence.

Patrik climbed the steps. Pressed the doorbell with the knuckle of his right hand. The button stuck slightly before it gave way with a dull electric ping. He adjusted his grip on the bag and waited. His stance said neighbourly visit. His eyes didn't. The tray had left a warm stripe against his palm, damp with condensation. He didn't move it.

From inside: footsteps. Slow, deliberate. Not hurried. The kind of pace that didn't apologize. He glanced sideways — flowerpots on either side of the door, one of them missing a petal. A faint chemical tang in the air, sharp against the late summer warmth. The lasagna shifted in its tray, heavy with good intentions.

He took a slow breath. It smelled like reheated food, pine cleaner, and control.

The door opened without a sound. Andreas Karlsson filled the frame — broad shoulders, sleeves rolled just enough to show forearms that didn't need to prove anything. His hair was damp, combed back. No smile, just the hint of one waiting if required.

"Patrik," he said, as if they'd spoken yesterday.

Patrik held up the bag, the lasagna now an offering. "Thought you and the girls could use this. Can't be easy with her taking off like that. Dumping the girls on you."

Andreas nodded slowly, eyes on the bag before meeting Patrik's gaze. "That's kind of you."

The words landed soft, practiced. His hand reached out — not hurried, not hesitant — taking the bag like it was expected. Behind him, the hallway stretched back in unnatural order. Shoes aligned. Coats zipped and buttoned on their hooks. No clutter. No life.

Further in, two small figures sat on a rug, wooden blocks arranged in precise rows rather than towers. Elsa glanced up first, then Maja. Neither spoke. Neither smiled. Just watched — waiting for nothing in particular.

Andreas followed Patrik's gaze but didn't comment. Instead, he shifted the bag to his left hand and leaned casually against the doorframe.

"Appreciate you thinking of us," he said, voice even. "It's been... a week."

Patrik nodded, the kind of nod that didn't agree or disagree. His eyes returned to the girls. Still no sound. No movement. The only noise was the faint creak of Andreas' knuckle against the plastic handle as his grip tightened — then eased.

The warm air carried a trace of something sharper now — ammonia beneath the smell of pasta and cheese.

"If there's anything else..." Patrik let the sentence trail off, knowing it didn't need finishing.

"We'll manage," Andreas said. Not defensive. Just definitive.

The bag sagged slightly in Andreas' hand, but he made no move to set it down. He stayed in the doorway, filling it without effort. The warm afternoon light caught on the edge of the door, casting a line between inside and out.

"It's been hard," Andreas said, his gaze steady but not inviting. "But we're managing."

Patrik nodded again, hands in his jacket pockets now — casual, as if he hadn't noticed the absence behind those words. The smell of food drifted out, mixing with the sharper scent beneath. Clean floors. Clean conscience.

"Girls seem quiet," Patrik said, his voice neutral.

Andreas didn't turn to look. "They know when to behave."

From the rug, Elsa shifted one block half a centimeter. Maja watched her sister, then returned her eyes to the floor. No whispers. No fidgeting. Just waiting for the moment to end.

The silence stretched, held politely in place by the doorframe between them. Andreas leaned his shoulder against it, the picture of a man holding things together — just a father doing his best.

"Sofia still not heard from?" Patrik asked, the question almost an afterthought.

"No," Andreas said, too quickly smooth. "But I'm sure she'll turn up when she's finished."

Another nod. Another silence. The threshold stayed firm — no invitation, no shift in weight that suggested one might come. A neighborly chat, nothing more.

Patrik glanced once more at the girls, then back to Andreas. The door didn't move. Neither did he.

Andreas shifted his weight, the floorboard inside giving a soft creak — the only sound between them now. Patrik's eyes drifted past him, as if by accident.

The hallway was too bright. The light from a ceiling fixture, not the sun. Shoes lined up with military precision — pairs too small and one pair too large, all pointing the same way. A jacket hung neatly on a hook, child-sized, zipper pulled all the way to the top.

The smell was clearer now. Not just cleaning product — something sharper, recent. Beneath it, the faint, sour trace of food reheated more than once.

Elsa sat perfectly still, hands resting on her knees. Maja copied her, though her fingers twitched against the fabric of her leggings before she caught herself. Their blocks weren't built into anything. Just sorted — by color, by shape. Order where there shouldn't be any.

Patrik let his gaze rest on the corner of a framed photo near the door. A family picture, but only half-visible from where he stood. The edge of a smile. A blurred park in the background. Faces turned inward, away from him now.

Andreas followed his line of sight, then straightened. The bag in his hand rustled softly as he adjusted his grip — a reminder of hospitality received and completed.

Patrik said nothing. There was nothing to ask that wouldn't already have an answer prepared.

The warmth of the afternoon pressed against his back. Inside, everything was too still, too clean — as if life had been scrubbed down to something manageable.

Andreas shifted first — a subtle lean forward that signaled the end without saying it. The lasagna hung heavy in his hand, the plastic handle stretched white where his fingers curled around it.

"Thanks again," he said, voice steady, almost warm. "Not everyone would've bothered."

Patrik gave a slight nod, already stepping back. The threshold stayed between them, unbroken.

But Andreas moved with him — just enough to reach out. His hand landed on Patrik's shoulder, firm and deliberate. Not a clap, not a pat. A grip.

The weight of it settled through the fabric of Patrik's jacket, fingers pressing with the kind of familiarity that wasn't earned. A pause held there — too long for politeness, too measured for friendship.

Andreas' eyes held his, the corners of his mouth tilting into something that might pass for gratitude. Or warning.

"Good to know we've got neighbors looking out for us," he said quietly, as if it were a compliment.

Patrik didn't step away. He waited. Let Andreas decide when to let go.

The release came slow, fingers uncurling like the end of a handshake no one had offered. Andreas stepped back into the doorway, the smile fading without fully leaving.

"Take care, Patrik."

The door didn't close yet. It just hovered — Andreas framed there, still holding the weight of the meal like a symbol of something understood but unspoken.

The door closed with a soft click behind him. No lock turning — none needed.

Patrik stood for a moment on the step, the warmth of Andreas' grip still faint on his shoulder. The late afternoon sun caught the edges of the gravel, casting long shadows that didn't belong to anyone.

He walked back to the car without hurry. Each step light, as if making noise might disturb something that had already settled too deep.

Empty-handed now. The weight of the lasagna gone, replaced by something heavier in the chest — nothing he could carry, nothing he could put down.

A bird called out again from the lilac bush. No answer this time either.

Patrik reached the driver's side, resting his hand on the roof for a moment before opening the door. The metal was warm under his palm — the only thing that offered any proof the sun was still shining.

He glanced once at the house. Curtains untouched. No movement. The kind of stillness that didn't break when watched.

Sliding into the seat, he shut the door with care. The engine didn't start right away. He sat there, fingers resting on the steering wheel, eyes on the road ahead but seeing none of it.

When he finally turned the key, the hum of the engine felt too loud against the silence he was leaving behind.

The car rolled forward, gravel crunching under the tires — the only sound marking his departure.

CHAPTER 4

Cecilia's Comfort

The churchyard smelled of cut grass and old stone. Cecilia stood by the gate, where the gravel met the worn path. Her dress was the kind that spoke of care — navy blue, buttoned high, sleeves just right for early summer. Not a hair out of place. Not a crease unplanned.

Patrik noticed the way her hands rested — one folded over the other, fingers still. Like she was posing for a photograph no one would take. Her gaze followed a pair of swallows darting above the spire, but her posture didn't soften. It never did.

He could have walked past. Pretended not to see her. But in Keldarp, that wasn't how things worked. He kept his pace steady, the weight of inevitability settling with each step.

Cecilia turned before he reached her. A small smile — polite, practiced. The kind that offered nothing.

"Patrik."

He nodded. No need for more.

The church bell marked the hour, hollow and distant. She didn't glance at the time. She already knew it.

For a moment, neither spoke. The breeze tugged at the hem of her dress, but she held firm — a figure carved from propriety and quiet judgment.

Her eyes settled on him, calm and measuring. Whatever conversation was coming, it wasn't chance. She had waited.

The bell's echo faded, leaving only the rustle of leaves against stone. Patrik shifted his weight, but Cecilia had already closed the distance — a step too close for comfort, just enough to make turning away impolite.

"Terrible business," she said, voice soft, almost tender. The kind of tone reserved for funerals and confessions.

Patrik didn't answer. His eyes drifted past her, to the church door left ajar. The faint scent of candle wax floated out — faint, but present.

"What kind of mother," Cecilia continued, "doesn't pick up her children?"

The words hung there. Not sharp, but placed with precision. She glanced toward the road as if expecting someone else to appear — a witness, perhaps, to her restraint.

Patrik's jaw tightened. He kept his gaze steady on a patch of gravel by her shoes — polished, low heels, the kind that didn't tolerate dirt yet stood in it anyway.

Cecilia sighed, a sound too controlled to be genuine. "We try to be understanding. But there are limits. Just disappearing like that. Dumping the girls on Andreas."

Her hand brushed invisible dust from her sleeve, a gesture that spoke louder than the words. She wasn't asking for agreement. She was offering a truth — the village's truth — neatly wrapped in concern.

Patrik let the silence answer. It said enough.

A cloud passed over the sun, muting the light. Cecilia straightened, as if the shift in weather signaled her cue.

"It wasn't just the children," she began, her voice low but steady. "You know Sofia refused to have them christened."

She didn't wait for a response. Her gaze was fixed somewhere beyond Patrik — the gravestones, perhaps, or the weight of tradition she carried like scripture.

"People whispered, of course. A mother turning her back on the Church… on what's right." Her lips pressed into a thin line, disapproval and disappointment folded into one expression.

Patrik kept still. The gravel beneath his boots felt softer than it should — worn down by years of feet treading the same path.

"And those trips," Cecilia continued, smoothing the front of her dress though it didn't need it. "All that travel for work. Always sales conferences, always somewhere far. A woman alone."

She let the implication settle, heavy but unsaid.

"And now…" Her eyes found his, calm and certain. "Andreas is left to pick up the pieces. Doing his duty, despite everything."

The breeze stirred again, lifting a strand of her hair before she tucked it back into place. Composure restored.

"Not everyone is made for responsibility," she added, softer now. "Some run from it."

Her words were smooth, polished by years of use — verdicts delivered as if they were kindnesses.

The church door creaked as a draft pushed it wider. Inside, the faint glint of brass candlesticks caught what little light remained. Cecilia's voice faded, but the echo of her words lingered heavier than the bell had.

Patrik stood unmoved. His hands rested by his sides, fingers curling once before relaxing again. He watched the edge of her glasses catch the sun as it reappeared — a sharp glint, gone as quickly as it came.

Cecilia didn't expect a reply. That wasn't the purpose. She looked past him now, to the graves lined in neat rows, names carved into stone that no one visited anymore.

The silence stretched. Not uncomfortable — practiced. In Keldarp, knowing when not to speak was a virtue.

A sparrow landed on the gatepost between them, its head twitching in quick, nervous movements. Cecilia glanced at it, then back to Patrik. Her expression softened, but only at the edges — satisfaction settling into place where judgment had been.

Patrik shifted his gaze to the horizon, where the trees marked the village's boundary. His face gave nothing away. Whatever passed between them wasn't conversation. It was confirmation.

The wind stilled. There was nothing left to hear.

Cecilia adjusted her handbag strap, a small, deliberate motion. The kind that signaled an ending without needing words.

"Well," she said, with a nod that carried the weight of conclusion. Her eyes swept over Patrik one last time — not searching, but confirming.

The sparrow took flight as she turned, its wings beating quick against the still air. Her heels found the familiar rhythm of gravel underfoot, each step measured, unhurried.

Patrik watched her cross the churchyard, posture straight, head high. The kind of walk reserved for those certain of being right.

The church bells had long gone silent, but their echo seemed to follow her — or maybe it was just the absence of anything else.

At the gate, she paused. Smoothed her skirt where it didn't need smoothing. Then she moved on, disappearing past the low stone wall, swallowed by routine.

Patrik stayed where he was. The faint scent of lilac drifted from somewhere near the graves, sweet but fading.

The approval she left behind hung heavier than accusation ever could. He felt it settle — quiet, persistent, like dust that never really cleared.

CHAPTER 5

Napoli at Dusk

The bell above the door gave a tired jingle as Patrik stepped inside. Same sound as always — thin, a little off-key, but enough to mark his arrival.

Napoli smelled of warm dough, melted cheese, and the faint bitterness of old fry oil. The kind of smell that settled into the walls, into clothes, into routine. A hum from the drinks fridge filled the quiet, steady and indifferent.

Aram glanced up from behind the counter. A nod — nothing more. Patrik returned it, already moving toward the corner where the takeout orders waited.

Tobbe's Volvo was parked outside. Patrik had seen it as he pulled in, knew what to expect before the door even swung shut behind him. Same as most evenings when the village started to dim and there wasn't much left to do but lean on old habits.

He let his eyes adjust to the warm light. Outside, daylight was fading — the kind of blue that made shop windows glow brighter than they should. Inside, the hum of appliances, and the low clink of glass on wood from the counter.

No one spoke. There wasn't any need. Patrik's boots made a soft sound against the worn floor as he moved further in. The bell's echo had already died, leaving the place settled back into its usual rhythm — quiet, familiar, unspoken.

Tobbe didn't turn when Patrik approached. He stayed leaned against the counter, one elbow resting on the wood, fingers loosely around a half-empty beer bottle. The label was peeling where his thumb had worked at it, absent-minded but steady.

"Late again," Tobbe said, eyes still on Aram, who was checking something on the till. His voice was casual, the kind used when words were just to fill space.

"Roadworks," Patrik answered, though he wasn't sure that's what Tobbe was talking about. A white box had his name scrawled across the top in black marker. He didn't reach for it yet. He let his hand rest on the edge of the counter, close enough to Tobbe's bottle to notice the condensation ring left behind.

Aram gave a small shrug without looking up. "Always something," he said. His Swedish flat but practiced, the kind that fit without ever sounding local.

Tobbe finally glanced at Patrik, a flicker of recognition passing between them — not surprise, just confirmation. Of course he was here. Same as always.

"Volvo's rattling again," Tobbe said, nodding toward the window where his car sat under the dim glow of the streetlamp. "Thinking it's the exhaust this time."

Patrik followed the nod but said nothing. The Volvo, an old 745, looked like it always did — tired, but holding together. Much like

Tobbe.

Aram wiped his hands on a cloth, watching the exchange without stepping into it. The quiet stretched, filled only by the soft hum of the fridge and the muted sound of a car passing by outside, too fast for the village speed limit.

"You'll sort it," Patrik said at last, voice low. Not advice. Just a fact.

Tobbe gave a short grunt that could've been agreement or dismissal. He lifted the bottle, took a slow sip, and let his gaze drift back to Aram, who was already turning away to check the oven.

The conversation settled into silence again, the kind that didn't need patching up. Outside, the last of the daylight faded, but inside Napoli, nothing pressed forward. Just the weight of familiar company and words that stayed where they belonged — unsaid.

Tobbe set his bottle down with a soft tap against the counter. The sound lingered longer than it should have. Aram slid a pizza box onto the warming shelf, his movements precise, uninterested.

Patrik reached for his box, fingers brushing the cardboard, but didn't lift it. Tobbe's eyes stayed on the worn surface of the counter, tracing invisible lines in the wood with his thumb.

"That bastard..." Tobbe's voice was quieter now, as if the words weren't meant to travel far. He didn't look at Patrik. Just kept his gaze fixed on nothing in particular. "Andreas."

Aram didn't react. If he heard, he gave no sign. The hum of the fridge filled the space where a response might have gone.

Tobbe shifted his weight, the stool creaking under him. His hand wrapped back around the bottle, but he didn't drink. The next words came out flat, like they'd been waiting too long to stay inside.

"Something's off. The girls…it's not right. He…you know…"

The words didn't ask for agreement. They didn't ask for anything. They just hung there, heavier than the warm air and the smell of oregano and melted cheese.

Patrik didn't move. The box stayed under his hand, untouched. His eyes stayed forward, fixed on the rows of scratch cards behind the counter, their bright colors dull in the fading light.

Aram wiped down the surface beside them, methodical, his presence neutral as always. The kind of neutrality that came from knowing when not to listen too closely.

Outside, the sky deepened into the last shade before dark. Inside, nothing shifted. The comment had been made — not loud, not dramatic. Just enough to let the truth breathe, if only for a moment.

Tobbe didn't wait for a reply. He took a slow pull from his beer, eyes fixed somewhere beyond the counter, where the neon OPEN sign flickered against the windowpane.

Patrik let the silence settle. He didn't shift, didn't clear his throat. Just stood there, the weight of Tobbe's words pressing into the space between them. His hand still rested on the pizza box, the warmth beneath his palm unnoticed.

When Tobbe finally glanced his way — a sideways look, brief and without expectation — Patrik met it. No words. Just a small, deliberate nod. Barely more than a movement, but enough.

Aram busied himself with the register, the faint beep of buttons punctuating the quiet. If he noticed the exchange, he gave no sign. Years behind that counter had taught him when to let things pass without acknowledgment.

The fridge hummed on. Somewhere in the back, the oven door clicked shut. Outside, a car rolled by, headlights sweeping across the window before disappearing down Road 46.

Tobbe set his bottle down again, lighter this time. The message had been delivered. In Keldarp, that was as close to truth as most people dared to get.

Patrik straightened slightly, fingers tightening around the edge of the box. The conversation, if it could be called that, was over. Nothing more needed saying. Nothing more could be said.

Tobbe drained the last of his beer in two steady gulps. No rush, just the practiced efficiency of a man who knew exactly how much time to give a moment before moving on.

He set the empty bottle down with a dull clink, pushed himself off the counter, and adjusted his jacket without looking at either of them. The stool scraped softly against the floor as it swung back into place.

"Aram," Tobbe said, a nod accompanying the name — more habit than farewell.

Aram returned it with the faintest lift of his chin, already wiping down a stack of menus that didn't need cleaning. Routine was its own kind of comfort.

Tobbe glanced at Patrik, but whatever passed through his mind stayed behind his eyes. He gave a short grunt — something between acknowledgment and dismissal — then turned toward the door.

The bell jingled as he stepped out, sharper now against the thickening quiet. Cool air rushed in for a moment before the door swung shut behind him, muting the world outside once more.

Through the window, Patrik watched Tobbe cross the patio, his shoulders hunched against the evening chill. The Volvo's door creaked open, then shut. The engine coughed to life, headlights cutting across the empty road before the car rolled away, swallowed by dusk.

Inside, the fridge hummed on. The smell of baked dough and tomato sauce lingered, unchanged. Aram moved in the background, steady as ever. The brief disturbance of truth had passed, leaving Napoli exactly as it had been before — quiet, warm, and waiting for the next familiar ritual to play out.

The bell's echo faded, leaving Patrik alone with the low hum of appliances and the quiet shuffle of Aram's movements behind the counter.

He didn't move straight away. The pizza box rested under his arm now, but his gaze drifted past the glass door, out to where the streetlights flickered against the deepening blue.

The neon sign buzzed faintly, its red glow bleeding onto the pavement. Beyond that, Keldarp was folding into itself — porch lights switching on, curtains drawn, engines cooling in driveways. The kind of silence that wasn't empty, just practiced.

Aram didn't speak. He wiped down a spotless counter, eyes down, giving Patrik the space without offering anything more.

Patrik watched as the last traces of daylight slipped behind the rooftops. The sky held that brief, in-between shade — not quite night, but with nothing left of day worth holding onto.

The village settled. A place that knew how to stay quiet, even when it shouldn't.

Patrik shifted his weight, fingers tightening around the box's edge. There was nothing keeping him there, but still he stood — letting the weight of what had passed hang in the warm air a moment longer.

When he finally turned toward the door, Aram simply nodded. No words exchanged. None needed.

The bell jingled again as Patrik stepped out into the cool air. Behind him, Napoli's lights glowed against the dark — a small island of warmth in a village that had already decided what it would and wouldn't see.

CHAPTER 6

The Daycare's Explanation

The gate creaked louder than necessary as Patrik pushed it open. Gravel shifted under his boots — the kind of sound that made heads turn in a village like this. Sebbe followed a step behind, adjusting his cap, the fabric of his uniform too crisp against the sagging fence and peeling paint of the daycare's entrance.

Inside, children's voices floated through an open window. High-pitched, careless. A different world. The kind where nothing stayed broken for long. Patrik let the sound pass over him, his hand resting on the door handle for a moment longer than needed.

The door swung open before he knocked. Anna, one of the nannies, stood there with a smile too wide for the situation. Floral blouse, hair pulled back tight, eyes darting between the two uniforms.

"We were expecting you," she said, stepping aside without waiting for a greeting.

Patrik nodded once and stepped in. The air smelled of dish soap and crayons. Sebbe offered a polite smile, his notebook already in hand, pen clipped and ready — eager, as always.

The hallway was lined with children's drawings. Suns with too many rays. Houses with no doors. Patrik's gaze lingered on a crooked figure — stick arms reaching out, faces drawn without mouths.

Anna led them to a small office, the kind where serious conversations were softened by pastel cushions and a bowl of wrapped candy no one touched. Another nanny, Erika, waited inside, her hands folded too neatly in her lap.

"We just want to help," Anna said, sitting down opposite them. Her voice carried that rehearsed lightness — the kind people used when pretending things were fine.

Patrik didn't answer. He let Sebbe take the chair beside him, let the silence stretch until Erika shifted in her seat and reached for the candy, thinking better of it halfway.

The chairs scraped softly against the linoleum as they settled in. The hum of a distant washing machine filled the gaps where conversation should have been. Anna glanced at Erika, who gave a small nod — the kind that passed for courage here.

"It was late," Anna began, smoothing the crease in her skirt that wasn't there. "Fridays are always... hectic."

Patrik watched her hands. Not the face — hands told more truth. Fingers fidgeted with a bracelet, cheap silver catching the light. Sebbe scribbled something, the scratch of pen on paper louder than Anna's voice.

"Andreas had a note," Erika added, almost too quickly. "From Sofia."

Neither of them looked at Patrik when they said it. The name hung in the room like a draft. He shifted slightly, letting the weight of his uniform do the talking.

"We know him," Anna continued, forcing a smile that didn't ask for approval. "It's not like he's a stranger."

Outside, a child laughed — sharp and sudden. Erika flinched before catching herself. Sebbe glanced up, pen hovering.

"The note," Patrik said, the first word he'd offered since sitting down.

Anna reached into a drawer without hesitation. A folded paper appeared, edges worn from being handled too often for something so supposedly routine. She placed it on the table, fingers lingering a moment before pulling back.

"It's from Sofia," she said, almost as if reassuring herself.

Patrik didn't answer. He unfolded the note slowly, eyes scanning the familiar loops of a signature he'd never seen in person. The paper smelled faintly of hand lotion and something else — something harder to place.

The note lay open between them, its presence already shrinking under the weight of normality. Erika leaned back, arms crossed loosely — not defensive, just done with the subject.

"We were a bit shocked when Andreas showed up. You know with the court order," Anna said, voice lighter now. "But what should we do. He had the note."

Sebbe nodded, pen moving again. Routine. Dates. Names. No hesitation.

"It's not the first time she's late," Erika added, eyes drifting to the window where children's jackets swayed on hooks. "She works a lot. Always one of the first in the mornings. One of the last in the evenings."

Patrik didn't respond. He ran a thumb over the paper's edge — too smooth, too clean. But the words were simple. Practical. No flourishes. The kind of message that didn't invite questions.

Sebbe reached for the note, but Patrik kept his hand there a second longer before letting it go. He folded it carefully, tucking it into his notebook. Routine. Just in case they would open a case file.

"Anything else?" Erika asked, already half-turned toward the door. The conversation, in their minds, had ended before it began.

Sebbe glanced at Patrik, waiting. Patrik stood without a word, the chair legs scraping again — louder this time.

The hallway felt narrower on the way out. Children's voices echoed sharper now, the scrape of plastic toys against linoleum filling the spaces where conversation had been.

Sebbe paused by the door, flipping his notebook closed with a soft snap. He tapped the pen against the cover, glancing back toward the office.

"Got what we need," he said, more to himself than to Patrik.

Patrik adjusted his belt, gaze fixed on a row of tiny shoes lined up beneath a bench — mismatched, scuffed, some missing laces. A pink sneaker leaned against a worn-out boot, both waiting to be claimed by someone too young to understand paperwork.

Sebbe held the door open, letting in a gust of early summer air thick with cut grass and distant traffic. He squinted against the light, the brim of his cap offering little shade.

"Standard stuff," Sebbe added, stepping outside. "Late pick-up, note from home. Happens more than you'd think."

Patrik didn't answer. He followed, the door clicking shut behind them — a sound that belonged to routines, not warnings.

Sebbe put the pen in it's holder on the notebook. He looked up, waiting for Patrik to lead the way back to the car.

The car doors shut with a dull thud, swallowing the last of the daycare's noise. Sebbe started the engine, the radio crackling to life with muted voices before he switched it off again.

Patrik sat back, eyes on the windscreen but seeing nothing of the narrow street ahead. The note still pressed against his thoughts — not the words, but how easily they had been accepted. Paper and ink standing in for trust.

Sebbe drummed his fingers on the steering wheel, relaxed. Another task done. Another box ticked.

"Smooth enough," Sebbe said, glancing over. "Doesn't seem like anything to worry about."

Patrik's hand rested on his thigh, fingers tapping once — a silent rhythm of doubt. The breeze outside stirred the dust along the curb, lifting a plastic bag that danced for a moment before catching on a fence post.

He didn't speak. There was nothing to correct in Sebbe's words — not yet. Just that lingering weight in his chest, the kind that didn't fit into reports or procedures.

Sebbe shifted into gear, the car rolling forward as if the matter was settled. Patrik let it happen, his gaze following the line of hedges blurring past the window.

The note was with them. The girls were back with their father. And everything — on paper — in order.

CHAPTER 7

Tomas' Careful Words

The church door resisted, swollen by the early summer damp. Patrik pushed it open with a quiet scrape of wood on stone. The smell inside was familiar — old hymn books, candle wax, and something floral that didn't quite mask the scent of time.

He didn't bother with a songbook. Just found a place halfway back, where the pew creaked under his weight but no one turned to look. They knew him now. The cop who sat through sermons without folding his hands.

Up front, Andreas Karlsson's broad shoulders filled the space of two men. Head bowed, still as the stone font beside him. Elsa and Maja sat next to him. Too young for sermons, but silent and still. Well behaved. Well dressed.

Tomas stepped up to the pulpit with the ease of routine. His collar slightly askew, glasses sliding down his nose. He didn't clear his throat. Just began, voice steady, words chosen like stones placed carefully in a riverbed.

Responsibility. Community. Stepping up when others falter. Forgiveness for old sins. Second chances. The strength of a father doing his duties when the mother fails hers.

No names. No need.

Patrik watched the dust motes dance in a shaft of sunlight cutting through stained glass. The colors bled across the wooden floor — red, gold, and a sickly green.

A cough echoed from the back. Someone shifted in their seat. The usual murmurs of a congregation hearing what they wanted to hear.

Andreas didn't move. Not once.

The sermon flowed on — smooth, unbroken. Like the village itself. A surface undisturbed, even when the water ran dark underneath.

The benches groaned as people stood. Hymnals closed with soft thuds, a few voices lingering on the last note before fading into shuffling feet and polite nods. The service was over, but no one rushed. There was comfort in the slow gathering of coats and handbags, in the quiet exchanges that filled the space where faith, or at least the rituals of faith, had been spoken.

Patrik remained seated. Watching Tomas descend from the pulpit, his expression unchanged — neither proud nor burdened by the words he'd delivered. Just careful. Always careful.

Andreas rose at the front, deliberate in his movements. He shook Tomas' hand — a firm grip, a slight incline of the head. The gesture of a man acknowledged. A few parishioners offered pats on the back, murmured something that didn't carry. Andreas accepted it all with the calm of someone who knew his role was secure.

Patrik let his gaze drop to the worn grooves in the pew ahead. Fingertips tracing the initials carved there decades ago, when belief had more to do with boredom than salvation.

The organist began packing away sheet music. A child's laugh echoed briefly before being hushed by a mother's hand.

Outside, through the arched window, the sky was too bright for the weight in the room. Early summer sun, indifferent and clear.

Tomas lingered near the altar, exchanging final words with those who sought them. His eyes never drifted toward Patrik. Whether by intent or habit, it was hard to tell.

Patrik stood only when the church had thinned out. No need to join the slow procession toward the coffee urn yet. Better to let the words settle where they belonged — in the spaces between what was said and what everyone already decided to believe.

The parish hall smelled of overbrewed coffee and almond cake. Cups clinked against saucers, low conversation filling the gaps where the sermon had left off. Patrik stood near the window, the porcelain warm in his hand, untouched.

Tomas drifted through the room with practiced ease — a nod here, a quiet word there. The collar still visible beneath his sweater, marking him as both part of the crowd and apart from it.

When their eyes finally met, there was no invitation. Just a subtle tilt of Tomas' head toward a corner table, half-shadowed and away from the murmurs.

Patrik followed, footsteps muffled by the worn rug. They sat without greeting. The scrape of chairs louder than necessary.

Tomas sipped his coffee first, eyes on the steam rising between them.

"Thoughts on the sermon?" His voice was light, but the question hung heavier than the air around them.

Patrik let the silence stretch. A faint knock from a loose windowpane marked the seconds. He set his cup down, still full.

"Clear enough," he said.

Tomas' mouth twitched — not quite a smile, not quite regret. He looked past Patrik, watching Cecilia hold court by the cake table, her gestures precise, her approval doled out like communion.

"People need reminders," Tomas said quietly. "About trust. About second chances."

Patrik didn't answer. His gaze fixed on the thin crack running through the tabletop varnish — a line too straight to be accidental, too old to matter now.

The hum of conversation grew as more chairs scraped back, plates refilled. The village settling into its version of peace.

Tomas shifted in his seat, as if to say more, but found nothing useful. Patrik spared him the effort by standing first.

No goodbyes. Just a nod, and the weight left behind on the chair.

The sun hit harder outside, bleaching the gravestones and casting sharp shadows along the path. Patrik didn't head straight for his car. He let the gravel crunch beneath his boots, the sound steady, giving Tomas time to catch up — if he chose to.

He did. The soft tread behind him, closing the distance without urgency.

They stopped near the edge of the churchyard, where the trimmed hedge gave way to open road. The village stretched beyond — still, quiet, pretending nothing had been said inside those walls.

Tomas cleared his throat, hands buried deep in his pockets. His gaze stayed fixed on the horizon, where the fields blurred into forest.

"It's not about ignoring," he said. "It's about... holding things together."

Patrik watched a blackbird hop between the graves, head twitching at every movement. He said nothing.

"People need to believe in... the possibility of change," Tomas continued, voice lower now. "If we take that away, what's left?"

A breeze stirred the birch leaves above them, the rustle too soft to cover the strain in Tomas' words.

Patrik shifted his weight, eyes still on the bird as it took flight — startled by nothing at all.

"I know about the accusations. But we have to give him a chance," Tomas offered, almost as if seeking permission.

Patrik's jaw tightened, but he didn't speak. The silence said enough — and too much.

Tomas exhaled through his nose, a sound closer to defeat than relief. His hands stayed in his pockets as he nodded to himself, as if agreeing with a conversation only he could hear.

The village bell tower marked the hour — a single, hollow chime that drifted over the rooftops and faded into nothing. Tomas shifted beside him, the weight of unsaid words pressing down heavier than the sun on their backs.

He glanced at Patrik, searching for something in the lines of his face. Understanding, maybe. Or forgiveness.

Patrik kept his eyes on the road, where a lone Volvo passed by, its engine barely audible. The driver didn't look their way. No one ever did when there was nothing left to see.

Tomas' foot scraped against the gravel, a restless gesture that didn't suit him. He opened his mouth as if to add more, then closed it again — lips pressed thin, resigned to the silence between them.

Patrik didn't offer relief. He let the quiet settle, let Tomas carry the discomfort of hearing his own justifications echo back at him without challenge.

A dog barked somewhere in the distance. A door shut. Life continuing with the same determined blindness that filled the pews every Sunday.

When Tomas finally gave a small nod and turned away, it wasn't dismissal. It was acceptance — of a conversation that had ended long before it began.

Patrik remained a moment longer, watching the empty street, the clean facades hiding cracks no sermon could plaster over.

The sun had climbed higher by the time Patrik reached his car. Heat pressed through the windshield, the interior stale with the faint scent of old upholstery and dust. Sat there for a few moments.

In the side mirror, Tomas was a shrinking figure, already absorbed back into the churchyard — exchanging polite nods with a couple lingering by the gate. His posture was relaxed, the weight of their conversation folded neatly away like his sermon notes.

Patrik rolled down the window. The air outside wasn't much cooler, but it carried the sounds of Keldarp returning to routine — a lawnmower sputtering to life, distant laughter from a garden, the soft hum of a tractor somewhere beyond the houses.

Patrik tapped his fingers against the steering wheel, the rhythm uneven, then let his hand fall to his lap. There was nothing left to say — not here, not now.

The engine turned over with a reluctant growl. He eased the car onto the narrow road, tyres crunching over gravel before meeting the smooth indifference of asphalt.

In the rearview mirror, the church spire receded, framed by birch trees and cloudless sky. A landmark for those who needed direction — or a place to hide behind familiar words.

Patrik didn't glance back again. The village had already decided what it wanted to believe. And Tomas, like the rest, knew how to live with it.

CHAPTER 8

Majvor's Silence

The gravel shifted under Patrik's boots as he stepped onto the path. The yellow house stood quiet against the overcast sky, its paint dulled by years but holding on. Curtains drawn just enough to let the day in without inviting it.

He raised his hand to knock. Barely touched the wood before the door opened — no sound, no surprise. Majvor stood there, small and steady, as if she'd known the exact moment he'd arrive.

She didn't speak. Just held the door wider, enough for him to pass. The smell of coffee drifted out, mingling with the warm air heavy with the promise of rain.

Patrik gave a nod — more to the threshold than to her — and stepped inside. The door closed behind him with a soft click. No questions. No need.

His jacket found its place on the familiar hook. Shoes lined up beside a pair of well-worn slippers. The quiet between them wasn't empty — it was known. A kind of refuge that didn't ask for explanations.

Majvor moved ahead, her footsteps absorbed by the old wooden floor. Patrik followed, the weight in his chest easing with each step toward the kitchen.

The kitchen greeted him like it always did — dim light filtered through lace curtains, settling over worn surfaces that didn't pretend to be anything they weren't. The faint hum of an old fridge, the soft creak of wood adjusting to the day.

Majvor didn't ask how he took it. She never had to. The pot was already warm, the routine older than the need for words. She reached for the cups — chipped but clean — and set them down with a quiet clink that filled the space more than conversation ever could.

Patrik sat where he always sat. Chair angled just enough to see the window but not the door. His hands rested on the table, fingers tracing the grain without thought.

Steam rose as Majvor poured. Slow, steady. The smell of coffee wrapped around them — bitter, grounding, real. She placed his cup in front of him without ceremony, then filled her own.

An LED candle flickered in the corner, its false flame steady against the fading afternoon. Outside, the sky hung low, pressing against the glass with a dull light that made everything inside feel heavier and safer at once.

Majvor sat down across from him. No glance exchanged. The ritual was enough.

The coffee had cooled enough to drink, but Patrik hadn't touched it. His fingers curled around the cup, drawing in the warmth like it might steady what couldn't be said outright.

Majvor waited. Not expectant — just present. Her gaze fixed somewhere beyond him, past the kitchen walls, where answers didn't matter.

Patrik's eyes stayed on the dark surface in his cup. A faint ripple where his thumb shifted against the handle.

"Something's… off," he said, voice low, like testing how the words felt in the room.

Majvor didn't move.

He let the silence settle before continuing, each word dragged from a place he hadn't wanted to visit today.

"Too neat. Too quiet." His thumb tapped once against the ceramic, then stopped. "People see what they want."

The LED candle flickered again, its artificial glow catching on the edge of a tin filled with biscuits no one reached for.

Patrik exhaled through his nose. The next words came slower. "Kids don't get that quiet on their own."

Outside, a branch scraped against the window — the wind picking up, or maybe just a reminder that the world didn't pause for suspicion.

He didn't say the name. Didn't need to. It hung there anyway, heavier than the air, heavier than the coffee in his hands.

The words faded, but the weight they carried stayed in the room. Patrik's gaze remained fixed on his cup, as if answers might form in the cold swirl of coffee.

Majvor lifted her cup, hands steady, the porcelain resting lightly between fingers that had known decades of holding things together. She took a sip — not rushed, not thoughtful. Just part of being there.

The quiet stretched, unbothered by the need to fill it. The creak of the house settling, the distant hum of a car passing through Keldarp — life continued its slow rhythm beyond the kitchen walls.

Patrik shifted in his seat, the chair giving a soft complaint. He didn't look up. There was nothing to meet — no judgment, no questions waiting in Majvor's eyes.

She set her cup down with care, the faint click on the tablecloth barely a sound at all. Her gaze found him then — calm, anchored — but she said nothing.

The LED candle flickered again, casting a weak glow that reached neither of them but marked the moment all the same.

Majvor's presence filled the space where words would have only gotten in the way. She listened without leaning forward, without nodding, without offering the comfort of clichés.

It was enough. More than enough.

The clock on the wall ticked, each second marking nothing urgent. Patrik finally lifted his cup, took a sip that had more to do with habit than thirst.

Majvor watched him — not searching, not weighing — just seeing him as he was. The kind of seeing that didn't require explanations.

When she spoke, it was without preamble. No lead-in. No softening.

"I trust you'll do what needs doing."

Her voice was steady, the words plain. Not reassurance. Not advice. Just a fact placed gently between them.

Patrik let the sentence settle. He didn't nod. Didn't thank her. The floor creaked as he shifted his weight, but otherwise, nothing moved.

Outside, the first drops of rain tapped against the window — sparse, hesitant. The kind of rain that didn't cool the air, only reminded you it could get heavier.

Majvor reached for her cup again, her attention already drifting back to the quiet rituals of the afternoon. The conversation, if it could be called that, was over before it had begun.

Patrik glanced at her then. Not for confirmation — he'd already been given all she had to offer. And it was enough.

The rain had settled into a steady patter by the time Patrik stood. The cups remained on the table, half-finished — as they often did.

Majvor didn't rise. She only watched as he reached for his jacket, the familiar weight of it slipping over his shoulders without fuss.

At the door, he paused. Hand on the handle, eyes on the blurred outline of the village beyond the glass. The air outside pressed heavy, warm and wet, but it felt thinner than when he'd arrived.

He glanced back, meeting Majvor's gaze for the first time since the words had passed between them. A small nod — more breath than movement.

"Thanks," he said. Barely audible, but it didn't need to be more.

The door opened with a soft groan. The porch creaked under his step as he stood for a moment, letting the rain touch his face, the weight of the kitchen left behind but not forgotten.

The sky hung low, but the burden sat differently now — not gone, just shifted enough to carry.

Patrik moved down the steps, the gravel damp beneath his boots. Behind him, the door closed quietly. No lock turned. No need.

CHAPTER 9

The File Opens

The corridor smelled of nothing. Just stale air, recycled too many times through vents no one cleaned often enough. The fluorescent lights buzzed overhead — steady, indifferent. Patrik's shoes made no sound on the worn linoleum, but he could hear the faint clatter of keyboards from somewhere deeper in the station. The low hum of a printer. A drawer sliding shut.

He passed the notice board without looking. The same memos had been pinned there for weeks — reminders about protocols no one enforced, posters about workplace wellness curling at the edges. Someone had left a coffee cup on the windowsill. The stain beneath it had dried into a perfect ring.

Patrik adjusted the strap of his bag on his shoulder. The weight wasn't much, but it pressed against him all the same. He reached the door to the office, pausing for a second as if expecting something different on the other side. It was a habit, not hope.

The handle was cool under his hand. He pushed it down, stepped inside.

More of the same light. More of the same air. Sebbe's head was bent over his desk, fingers tapping at a keyboard with the kind of focus only rookies still had. Across the room, the faint smell of burnt coffee lingered — someone had forgotten to turn off the machine again.

Patrik moved to his desk without a word. The chair creaked as he sat down. The monitor blinked awake, bathing his face in pale blue. A small reflection in the dark screen showed nothing he didn't expect — a man arriving to do what was required, no more, no less.

Elin stood by the filing cabinet, leafing through a folder with the kind of calm that came from knowing exactly what she'd find. The fluorescent light flattened everything — her hair tied back, the crisp lines of her shirt, the stack of papers in her hand. Patrik's chair gave a soft creak as he leaned back, eyes meeting hers for a moment. Nothing passed between them. Not yet.

She closed the folder and walked past his desk, her steps unhurried. No papers in her hand now. Just the air between them.

She paused beside him. Not facing him directly — just near enough that her voice didn't have to carry.

"You opening a case?"

Patrik's fingers hovered over the keyboard. He didn't look up.

"Yeah."

That was all. Elin moved on. The folder she'd taken landed on her own desk with a soft thud, its contents untouched. Across the room, Sebbe tapped out notes without looking up. The hum of the overhead lights returned, soft and constant.

Patrik typed the name. Sofia Karlsson-Lindqvist. The cursor blinked. The first field filled in.

The process had begun. No ceremony. Just work. Just what came next.

The form sat half-finished on the screen, cursor blinking without urgency. Patrik pushed his chair back, the wheels dragging slightly on the worn patch of floor beneath his desk.

Sebbe was hunched over a stack of reports, pen tapping against the edge of the paper in a restless rhythm. The kind of noise that filled silence without meaning to. Patrik stood for a moment, watching the back of the young officer's head — hair still neat from a morning routine that hadn't yet been worn down by years of this.

"We're opening a file," Patrik said, voice low, almost blending into the background hum.

Sebbe glanced up, pen freezing mid-tap. His eyebrows lifted — a flicker of something between curiosity and the instinct to be helpful.

"Sofia?"

Patrik nodded once. No explanation offered. None needed.

Sebbe leaned back in his chair, the plastic armrests creaking under the shift of weight. He let out a breath that tried to sound casual.

"Just procedure, right?"

Patrik's gaze held his for a second longer than necessary. Then he looked away, returning to his desk.

"Yeah."

The word sat there, thin and weightless. Sebbe didn't push further. His pen resumed its quiet tapping, but slower now — like he was keeping time with a thought he didn't want to finish.

Patrik sat down, the cursor still blinking where he'd left it. The office settled back into the familiar sounds of keys, paper, and the quiet pretence that routine could still mean something.

The tapping stopped. Sebbe's chair creaked once more as he shifted back to his paperwork. The room settled into a stillness that wasn't quiet — just filled with the low, constant hum of machines doing what they were built to do.

Patrik's fingers moved across the keyboard, steady and unhurried. Each keystroke felt heavier than it should. Letters forming a name that had already been spoken too often in hushed tones and knowing glances.

Sofia Karlsson-Lindqvist.

The system lagged for a moment — a small spinning circle at the center of the screen, as if even the software hesitated before committing. Then the case number appeared. Black text on a grey background. Clean. Efficient. Detached.

Patrik sat back, eyes on the number. A string of digits that now held what was left of her in official memory. The weight of it wasn't in the act, but in how familiar it all was. Another file. Another life reduced to forms and codes.

Elin didn't look up from her desk. Sebbe didn't ask if it was done. There was no need for announcements. The screen glowed in front of him, indifferent to what it carried.

Patrik reached for the mouse, clicked to save. The soft mechanical sound barely registered, but it marked the point where there was no turning back — not that there ever was.

The case number sat fixed on the screen. No urgency. No expectation. Just there — like it had always existed, waiting for someone to give it a name.

Patrik's hands rested on either side of the keyboard, fingers slightly curled but still. The faint warmth of the monitor touched his skin, a poor imitation of sunlight.

The office around him carried on — Elin turning a page, Sebbe scribbling something in the margins of a report. The familiar sounds of work being done because it was supposed to be done.

His eyes didn't move from the screen. Sofia's name, the date, the assigned number — all lined up in quiet order. A record of concern formalized too late to matter. The village had already closed this chapter in whispers and shrugs. He was just catching up.

The smell of burnt coffee drifted past again, sharper now. He didn't reach for a cup. There was no point.

Outside the window, nothing called for his attention. Inside, the cursor blinked in the next empty field, patient and indifferent.

Patrik stayed where he was, letting the weight of the process settle. Not fighting it. Just another line in a system built to acknowledge what everyone had already decided to forget.

CHAPTER 10

Procedure Begins

The folder sat heavier than it should. Thick paper edges worn soft from years of being handled, read, closed — but never acted on. The young caseworker flipped a page. Then another. Photocopies of bruises that had faded long before the ink dried. Statements rewritten until they meant nothing. Dates stacked like sediment, each layer burying the last.

Above, the fluorescent lights buzzed faintly. The kind of sound you stopped hearing after a while, but never really escaped. She adjusted in her chair, the vinyl seat sticking briefly to her skin where her blouse had ridden up. Outside, sunlight glanced off the windows — too bright for what sat in front of her.

A coffee cup stood near her elbow, half-full and cold. The surface film had started to wrinkle. She reached for it, then didn't. Her fingers traced the rim of the cup instead, eyes fixed on a paragraph detailing a "domestic disturbance" from two years ago. Language scrubbed clean — no mention of the way Sofia's voice had cracked on the phone. Just 'incident resolved on site.'

The copier in the hallway exhaled. A slow, mechanical sigh. Somewhere further off, muted voices traded something resembling laughter. She turned another page. A school report —

Elsa withdrawn, Maja unusually quiet for her age. Noted. Filed. Forgotten.

The young caseworker closed the folder for a moment, palm resting on the faded label. Andreas Karlsson. The name looked almost respectable in typed font. She knew it wouldn't matter how many pages were inside. The ending had already been decided — long before today.

She'd only been at Social Services a year. Long enough to see how cases ended. Not long enough to stop caring. That was the hard part.

Her thumb tapped the pen against the desk. Slow at first. Then quicker. The folder remained closed beneath her hand, but the words inside pressed against her skin like a pulse she couldn't ignore.

She glanced at the door — still ajar, the corridor empty. The soft whir of the copier had stopped. The office had settled into that familiar midday lull where nothing urgent ever happened, and everything important was quietly postponed.

The pen tapped again. A sharp, hollow sound against the laminate surface. She caught herself and set it down. Fingers curled into a fist instead, knuckles whitening as they pressed into the edge of the desk. Jaw tight. Breath held longer than needed.

The smell of stale coffee mixed with something sharper — Cecilia's perfume, lingering from when she'd passed by earlier. A scent too bright for this place. It clung to the air, invasive and out of place, like the words that would soon be written into the report.

She forced her hand open. Reached for the folder again but didn't lift it. The weight wasn't in the paper. It was in knowing exactly how this would end and that there wasn't a single thing she could do to stop it.

Outside the window, sunlight reflected off parked cars. Inside, the fluorescent light flattened everything. She sat back, staring at nothing, letting the frustration settle where it always did — low, dull, and useless.

The sound of footsteps softened against the office carpet before stopping at her desk. She didn't need to look up. The familiar weight of presence was enough. A hand, steady and deliberate, rested on the folder — fingers splayed just enough to signal ownership without force.

"Let's not get emotional."

The voice was calm. Practiced. No judgement, just routine. The young caseworker kept her eyes on the edge of the desk, where a faint scratch traced a line through the laminate. She nodded once, the kind of nod that didn't agree but didn't argue either.

The hand lingered on the folder, thumb brushing over the label as if smoothing out something that couldn't be seen. The fluorescent lights caught on the senior caseworker's wedding band — dull gold, worn thin at the underside. Another thing shaped by years of quiet pressure.

"People can change. People trust him."

The words landed without expectation. Not a conversation. Just protocol, spoken aloud to remind them both of the script. The young caseworker let her gaze drift to the window, where the sunlight had shifted, tracing a narrow line across the floor that never quite reached her desk.

The hand withdrew, taking the warmth with it. The folder remained. Closed. Waiting.

Footsteps retreated, swallowed by the hush of the office. She didn't move for a while. There was nothing left to say — and nothing left to do except follow the procedure.

The senior caseworker stopped by her desk again. No folder this time, just a glance that lingered a moment too long. "We've got the interviews today," she said. "Andreas is waiting. Some community names from Keldarp too." A pause. "Start with him."

The young caseworker nodded, stood, and smoothed her skirt. Her screen dimmed behind her as she followed the corridor toward the small interview room. Andreas was already seated when she arrived.

The chair creaked as Andreas Karlsson shifted his weight, settling into a posture that struck the balance between relaxed and respectful. Hands folded neatly on the table, shoulders squared but not tense. His eyes met theirs without hesitation — calm, clear, rehearsed.

The young caseworker sat opposite, pen poised but unmoving. The senior caseworker lingered by the door, arms crossed loosely, offering the kind of presence that said everything was under control.

"It's about stability," Andreas said, voice steady. "The girls need routine. Familiar faces."

His gaze didn't waver. The caseworker noted how his fingers tapped once against his wedding ring — still worn, despite the divorce. A small detail. Meaningless on paper.

The room smelled faintly of cleaning agents and the aftershave Andreas had chosen carefully that morning. Neutral. Respectable. The kind of scent that left no impression.

He spoke again, words flowing smoothly. Acknowledging past mistakes without dwelling. Emphasizing growth, responsibility, the importance of keeping his daughters in a stable environment. The phrases came easily — too easily.

The caseworker wrote a few lines. Not the truth. Just what was said.

Andreas offered a small smile as he finished. The kind that suggested humility, but held nothing behind it. His hands remained folded. No fidgeting. No signs of strain. Just a man playing his part — and playing it well.

The silence stretched, but he didn't fill it. He didn't need to.

The chairs hadn't cooled from Andreas when Cecilia Lövgren took her seat. Upright, hands resting lightly on her lap, as if the outcome depended on posture alone. The sharp scent of her perfume filled the small room, cutting through the lingering trace of Andreas' aftershave.

She didn't wait to be asked. Her voice, clear and measured, settled into the space with the confidence of someone accustomed to being heard.

"We all know the value of redemption," she began, eyes steady on the young caseworker. "Andreas has shown nothing but commitment to his duties as a father."

The caseworker's pen hovered above the notepad, reluctant. Across the table, Cecilia's gaze didn't flicker. There was no need for emphasis — every word already carried the weight of assumed agreement.

"Family unity," she continued, smoothing an invisible crease on her skirt. "That's what gives children the best chance. Stability. Familiarity. The community stands behind him."

Outside the window, a bird landed briefly on the sill before flying off. The caseworker watched it go, letting the words flow past — phrases polished by years of church meetings and council decisions.

Cecilia offered a small, composed smile. Not warm — purposeful. She glanced at the notepad, ensuring the right words were being captured. The caseworker wrote, though none of it felt necessary. The decision wasn't being made here. It had already been made — somewhere between tradition and expectation.

Cecilia folded her hands again, satisfied. The perfume lingered long after she stood to leave.

The door closed softly behind Cecilia, her perfume still hanging in the air when Tomas Nylander stepped in. He offered a polite nod, removing his cap and holding it loosely in both hands. His clerical collar peeked out from beneath a worn sweater — the uniform of someone trying to be approachable without forgetting who he was.

He sat without being asked, settling into the chair as if it were a parish bench. His eyes — kind, but tired — met the young caseworker's with something that resembled apology more than authority.

"Trust," he said quietly, as if the word itself might disturb the calm. "It's what holds us together."

The caseworker didn't lift her pen this time. Tomas wasn't here to convince — just to offer the gentle push everyone expected from him.

"We've all seen Andreas struggle," he continued, voice low, the cadence more sermon than statement. "But we've also seen him find his way back. Forgiveness isn't given because it's easy. It's given because we should — as we forgive those who trespass against us."

His thumbs rubbed the edge of his cap, tracing circles into the fabric. He glanced down at it, then back up, a soft sigh barely audible beneath the hum of the fluorescent lights.

"Second chances," he added, almost to himself.

The caseworker watched him for a moment, noting how his shoulders carried more than just the weight of this meeting. She wrote a single line — not because it mattered, but because silence didn't fit on the report.

Tomas offered a faint smile. Not of reassurance — but of someone who knew the difference between right and necessary, and had chosen the latter too many times.

The office was empty again. Afternoon light bled through the blinds in narrow stripes, but it didn't reach the desk where the young caseworker sat. The screen's glow flattened her face, casting shadows beneath tired eyes.

Her fingers moved across the keyboard without hesitation. The words came easily — they always did when meaning wasn't required. Phrases lifted from protocol, polished by habit. "Demonstrated commitment." "Stable environment." "Support from community representatives."

Each sentence smoothed the edges of what had been said in that room. Each word another layer of reassurance — not for the children, but for those who would read the report and nod, satisfied that the system worked.

The soft clatter of keys filled the space where frustration had been. There was no anger left now. Just procedure.

She paused, glancing at the folder still lying beside her. The history it contained wouldn't follow into this document — not really. It would sit there, quietly ignored, like it always had.

Her fingers resumed. A final paragraph. Confidence in the father's progress. The importance of continuity for Elsa and Maja. The decision had never been in question — only the wording.

She saved the file. Printed a copy. The printer hummed obediently, spitting out the pages that made it official.

Standing, she gathered the papers, aligning them neatly with a practiced tap against the desk. Outside, the bright day went on — indifferent.

She turned off her screen. The report lay ready for signature. Another case resolved — at least on paper.

CHAPTER 11

Sebbe's Optimism

Nattkröken never closed — not really. The lights stayed on, the grill stayed warm. Burgers, kebabs, pizza, the kind of food that left your fingers slick and your stomach heavy. On weekends, it filled up after last call — loud voices, smeared mascara, someone always crying by the bins. Weeknights were different. Take-out bags for shift workers. The occasional cab driver. A quiet table for two cops not ready to go home yet. The air smelled of old frying oil and sweet chili sauce. A fan buzzed above them, moving nothing.

The trays sat between them, catching the glare of the overhead lights. Grease pooled where the paper couldn't hold it back. A half-eaten burger in front of Sebbe, fries scattered like an afterthought. Patrik's meal untouched, cooling in the stale air of Nattkröken.

The hum of refrigeration filled the silence between words. Somewhere behind the counter, a timer beeped and was ignored.

"Should've clocked out earlier," Sebbe muttered, peeling back the wrapper from his second burger. "Bet Elin's still at her desk, though."

Patrik picked up a fry. It bent in his fingers, limp with oil. He set it down again.

Outside, neon reflected in puddles that hadn't dried despite the hour. Summer nights like these — cool, damp, lingering.

"Could've been worse," Sebbe said, mouth half-full. "At least it wasn't another domestic. Just paperwork and idiots."

Patrik nodded, eyes on the condensation sliding down his soda cup. Routine. The comfort of knowing what came next — burger, banter, bed.

"These fries are shit," Sebbe added, pushing them around with a finger before giving up. He leaned back, stretching until his joints popped. "Same crap every night, huh?"

Patrik let a small sound escape — not quite agreement, not quite disagreement. Just enough to keep the air from settling too heavy.

Their uniforms were gone, swapped for civilian jackets draped over the plastic seats. But the weight of the shift still clung to them — the kind that didn't wash off with a quick change of clothes.

Sebbe reached for his drink, the straw scraping against the lid. He slurped loudly, then grinned like it was a victory over the machine.

Patrik finally took a bite of his burger. It tasted like salt and routine. Across from him, Sebbe filled the space with easy complaints — about overtime, about Elin, about the coffee machine at the station that always jammed.

The kind of talk that kept darker thoughts at bay. At least for one more night.

Sebbe pushed his tray back with a sigh, the plastic scraping against the table's surface. He leaned forward, elbows planted, fingers absently tearing at the corner of a napkin.

"You know," he said, eyes flicking up, "I've been thinking about that mess with Karlsson."

Patrik didn't look up. He folded what's left of his burger wrapper into a tighter square, pressing the edges flat with his thumb.

"Social services will sort it," Sebbe continued, voice lighter than the words deserved. "They always do. That's what they're there for."

The hum of the refrigeration unit answered him. Patrik reached for his drink, letting the straw rest against his lower lip without taking a sip.

"I mean, they've got procedures for this stuff," Sebbe went on, warming to his own reassurance. "Court orders, evaluations... It's all in place. People screw up, sure, but the system knows how to handle it."

He smiled, like saying it made it true. The torn napkin twisted tighter in his hands.

"And Andreas — he's showing he wants to do right by his kids. That counts for something."

Patrik's gaze stayed on the condensation pooling beneath his cup. A drop traced a slow path along the table's edge before falling out of sight.

Sebbe waited, as if expecting agreement. When none came, he shrugged, the movement casual, dismissing any need for doubt.

"These things sort themselves out," he said, final now. Confident. Young.

Patrik set his cup down without a sound. The table between them felt heavier than it had a moment ago.

Sebbe picked up his burger again, gesturing with it as if the weight of it could carry his thoughts further.

"Tomas said it best on Sunday," he said, a smear of sauce near his thumb. "Everyone deserves a chance to prove they've changed."

He took a bite, chewing slowly, eyes somewhere past Patrik's shoulder — seeing something easier than the truth.

"Andreas... he's got the girls now. Maybe that's what he needed. A reason to straighten out."

Patrik's fork traced idle lines through the remaining fries, pushing them into neat rows only to scatter them again.

"People mess up," Sebbe continued, voice softer now, almost reflective. "But if no one trusts them to get better, what's the point?"

The burger hovered in Sebbe's hand, forgotten mid-gesture. He glanced at Patrik, searching for agreement, for that shared belief in something clean and simple.

Patrik didn't meet his gaze. His eyes stayed on the tray, on the grease stains spreading like quiet truths no one wanted to name.

Sebbe let out a small laugh — too bright for the hour, too certain. "Tomas believes in him. So does half the village."

He set the burger down, wiping his hands on the thin paper napkin that did little against the residue.

"You'll see," he added, almost as an afterthought. "This'll turn out fine."

Patrik shifted his weight, the chair creaking beneath him. The only response was the soft crumple of paper in his hand.

Sebbe's words faded, leaving only the low buzz of fluorescent lights and the distant hiss from the fryer no one was tending.

Patrik stared at his fries. Cold now, edges darkened, limp in a way that matched the hour.

Sebbe shifted in his seat, the movement restless. He drummed his fingers against the tray, a quiet rhythm to fill the space Patrik wouldn't.

"You think I'm wrong?" Sebbe asked, the question light, almost playful — as if daring Patrik to challenge him.

Patrik picked up a fry, turned it between his fingers, then set it back down. His jaw tightened, but no words followed.

Sebbe gave a short breath through his nose, half a laugh, half a shrug. "Didn't think so," he said, mistaking silence for agreement.

The napkin pile had become a crumpled mess in Sebbe's hands. He balled it up and tossed it onto the tray, leaning back with a satisfied nod — like the conversation had resolved something.

Patrik's eyes stayed on the tray between them. The smear of ketchup, the cooling meat, the weight of routine covering what neither of them wanted to name.

Outside, a car passed, its headlights dragging long shadows across the tiled floor before vanishing.

Sebbe checked his phone, the screen lighting up his face for a moment. "We'll see," he muttered, more to himself now.

Patrik didn't move. The quiet was easier than explaining what Sebbe wasn't ready to hear.

Sebbe wiped his hands, the thin napkin barely holding against the grease. He tossed it onto the tray, then stood, stretching like the day hadn't already worn him down.

"Let's see what tomorrow brings," he said, the words light, almost cheerful.

Patrik stayed seated, his fingers resting on the edge of the tray. The fries were untouched, the soda nearly full. He watched as condensation traced lazy lines down the plastic cup, pooling where it had nowhere else to go.

Sebbe grabbed both trays, stacking them with a clatter that echoed too loud in the empty space. He nodded toward the bins by the door.

"You coming?"

Patrik nodded, but didn't move right away. Sebbe took that as answer enough and walked off, his footsteps quick, unbothered.

The door swung open, letting in a draft of humid night air before closing behind him. Neon reflections shivered across the floor tiles, then stilled.

Patrik exhaled through his nose, slow and steady. He rose, dragging his chair back with a scrape that set his teeth on edge.

Outside, Sebbe was already by the car, keys in hand, looking up at the clear night like it promised something.

Patrik stepped into the damp air, letting the door shut behind him without a glance back. Sebbe was smiling — the kind of smile that hadn't learned yet what it would cost.

Patrik said nothing as he walked to the car. Some things didn't need to be corrected. Not tonight.

CHAPTER 12

Cecilia's Campaign

The smell of coffee hung in the air, thick and familiar. A tray of cinnamon buns sat at the center of each table, their sugar crystals catching the warm light from overhead lamps. Porcelain cups clinked against saucers, a quiet rhythm beneath the low murmur of conversation.

Patrik stood just inside the doorway, the edge of the room pressing against his back. The village hall looked the same as it always had — beige walls, laminated tables, chairs that creaked when someone shifted their weight. Comfortable in the way only routine could make it.

He moved to a corner table, nodding at no one in particular. A cup was already waiting — someone always made sure there was enough coffee. He wrapped his hands around it, letting the heat settle into his palms. Across the room, villagers leaned in over pastries and half-finished sentences, their voices soft but steady.

The monthly coffee hour had been announced after Sunday's service. Tomas called it a chance to reconnect. Others called it tradition. Patrik hadn't intended to come. He was still unsure why he had.

Cecilia's laugh floated above the rest. Not loud — just placed carefully enough to be noticed. She stood near the far table, a hand resting lightly on a neighbour's shoulder, her posture open and reassuring. The kind of presence that made people lean closer without realizing it.

Tomas lingered by the doorway, fingers tapping against his thigh, eyes scanning the room but never settling. When Patrik caught his gaze, Tomas offered a brief nod before looking away, as if acknowledging something neither of them intended to name.

The warmth in the room wasn't from the coffee or the lights. It was the practiced comfort of people who knew how to gather without saying too much. The kind of gathering where stories were shared without ever needing to be true.

Patrik sipped his coffee. It was just bitter enough to remind him where he was.

Cecilia's steps were slow, measured. A hand here, a nod there — never hurried. She moved between tables like she belonged to each of them, her presence settling over conversations without interrupting them.

Patrik watched as she leaned in toward Åke Jönsson, her hand resting lightly on the back of his chair. Her voice was low, but the kind that carried just enough to be heard by those nearby. Åke's shoulders eased as he listened, his fingers tracing the rim of his coffee cup.

"We must stand by those who take responsibility." The words slipped out of her with practiced ease, soft enough to sound like kindness. Åke nodded before she was even done speaking.

She straightened, offered a small smile, and moved on. Each stop the same — a brief touch, a quiet word, the reassurance of shared understanding. No persuasion needed when the script was already written.

At the far end, Karin Svensson reached for another bun as Cecilia approached. The two women exchanged a glance that said more than the murmured words that followed. Patrik couldn't hear them, but he didn't need to.

Tomas shifted by the wall, his hand now tucked into his pocket. His gaze followed Cecilia, but dropped whenever she turned his way.

Cecilia paused near the coffee urn, refilling her cup without rush. She scanned the room — not to admire it, but to take stock. When her eyes met Patrik's, she held the look for a moment longer than politeness required. Then came the smallest tilt of her head, as if to say this was how things were done.

Patrik let the silence answer for him. The coffee had gone cold in his hands, but he didn't move.

Cecilia's chair barely made a sound as she sat, folding her hands neatly around her cup. The group around her leaned in without being asked — drawn by the quiet gravity she carried.

The murmur of the room softened, not into silence, but into something more attentive. Spoons stirred coffee absentmindedly. A chair scraped against the floor in the corner. Routine sounds, shielding what came next.

Cecilia's eyes lowered, her fingers tracing the handle of her cup. When she spoke, it was almost a sigh.

"It came to me during prayer..." She let the words hang, soft and reverent. A pause, as if giving space for grace to settle in.

Across the table, Karin's brow furrowed — expectant, but not intrusive. Others watched with the same careful patience, the kind reserved for things that mattered but shouldn't be said too loudly.

"Spain," Cecilia continued, her voice touched with something like sorrow. "A man."

The details were few, but enough. A shared glance passed between two of the older women. Someone exhaled through their nose — not quite disapproval, not quite surprise.

Cecilia didn't elaborate. She didn't need to. The weight of her words wasn't in what she said, but in how gently she'd offered it. As if Sofia's absence had been explained by providence itself.

Patrik caught Tomas shifting again by the doorway, his head bowed slightly now, as if studying the floor. His mouth pressed into a thin line, but he stayed where he was.

The story had taken root. Not loudly, not crudely — just enough to feel inevitable.

Cecilia lifted her cup, blew lightly on the surface, and took a sip. The conversation around her resumed, softer than before, carrying her truth with it.

The clinking of cups masked the shift. Conversations dipped into safer topics — the weather, the price of petrol — but only on the surface. Beneath it, Cecilia's words settled like dust, unnoticed until they coated everything.

She leaned slightly toward Karin, voice low but clear enough for nearby ears. Her eyes cast down, as if reluctant to speak.

"Some are calling her a slut..." The words came with a soft shake of her head, the kind reserved for disappointments too grave to name outright.

Her fingers brushed a crumb from the table, a small, precise gesture. Then, almost as an afterthought — "I'd never say it myself."

Karin's lips pressed together, a faint nod following. Across the table, Åke avoided looking up, his hand busy folding a napkin that didn't need folding.

No one challenged it. No one needed to. The cruelty was wrapped so tightly in concern that unwrapping it would seem rude.

Cecilia let the silence fill the space where protest might have been. She sipped her coffee again, eyes still lowered — the picture of reluctant messenger.

Patrik watched the slow erosion happen in real time. One word, softly spoken, doing more damage than any shouted accusation could. The room didn't flinch. It absorbed.

Tomas had turned his back now, pretending to study the notice board by the door. His shoulders were stiff, his hands clasped behind him like a schoolboy waiting for a lesson to end.

Cecilia glanced around the table once more, offering a faint, regretful smile. The kind that said some truths were unfortunate — but necessary.

The room settled into a quiet hum, the kind that followed when everything that needed saying had been said — without anyone truly saying it.

Cecilia adjusted her glasses, her gaze drifting over the familiar faces. She didn't speak again. She didn't have to.

Karin reached for her cup, nodding slowly, eyes fixed on the tablecloth. Åke gave a small grunt of agreement, more habit than thought. Across the room, others mirrored the motion — subtle nods, murmurs too soft to carry meaning but loud enough to signal alignment.

"Poor girls..." someone muttered, a woman near the window. The words floated across the room, met with a few quiet affirmations. Another voice, lower, added — "At least they have their father."

Patrik let his eyes drift across the gathering. No raised voices, no debate. Just the comfort of a story everyone could live with. Easier to pity than to question.

Chairs shifted as people settled deeper into their routines — reaching for another bun, refilling coffee, exchanging glances that confirmed they all understood the same version of events now.

Cecilia folded her hands in her lap, her expression serene. The work was done, though it never looked like work. Just a village agreeing on what was best — for the children, for the community, for peace.

Tomas hadn't moved from his place by the door. His head was still bowed, but now his hand rubbed at the back of his neck, as if trying to ease a weight that wouldn't lift.

Patrik stayed where he was, cup untouched. The smell of coffee and cinnamon had gone stale in his nose, replaced by something heavier — the quiet finality of consensus.

The voices blended into a low, steady murmur — the sound of a village settling into its chosen version of events. No sharp edges, no doubts voiced aloud. Just the comfort of agreement.

Patrik remained seated, the weight of his presence unnoticed or politely ignored. His cup sat cold on the table, untouched since Cecilia's words began weaving their way through the room.

He let his gaze drift, not focusing on anyone in particular. The familiar faces blurred into a single expression — calm, content, certain.

Cecilia's laughter returned, softer now, threaded with the ease of a conversation that had moved on. The names and stories would follow their usual paths — winding through kitchens, passing over fences, settling into the walls of the village like damp.

Patrik didn't move. There was nothing to say, and no one expecting him to say it. His role here was clear — to observe, to understand when speaking would only make him an outsider again.

The warm light above him did little to soften the weight in his chest. It wasn't anger. It wasn't surprise. Just the quiet recognition that truth had no place in this room tonight.

Tomas stood near the door, still facing away. Patrik didn't call to him. There was no point.

The smell of coffee lingered, mixing with the faint sweetness of cinnamon and something harder to place — the stale air of stories that would never be questioned again.

Patrik exhaled through his nose, steady and slow. Then he looked down at his hands, resting flat against the table, and waited for the evening to end.

The chairs scraped back in slow succession, the signal that it was time to leave. Plates were gathered, cups stacked — the quiet choreography of people who knew their part.

Tomas remained by the doorway, his hand resting on the frame as if it anchored him. He didn't speak to anyone. When a couple passed him on their way out, he offered a faint smile without meeting their eyes.

Cecilia stood near the center of the room, exchanging final words with those still lingering. Her tone was light, almost cheerful — the kind reserved for a job well done. She straightened a stack of napkins, adjusted a tray, small gestures of order reinforcing control.

Patrik rose from his chair, slow and deliberate. He didn't cross the room. There was nothing left to witness.

Tomas caught his movement but didn't move himself. His gaze stayed fixed on a spot somewhere beyond the floorboards, his posture careful, as if still deciding whether to stay invisible or step forward.

The last of the villagers drifted out, their voices fading into the evening air. Cecilia's footsteps echoed softly as she walked toward the kitchen, humming under her breath.

Tomas finally shifted, his shoulders sinking as if whatever held them upright had been released. He glanced toward Patrik but looked away just as quickly — no words, no acknowledgment. Just the weight of knowing and choosing not to carry it further.

Patrik paused at the threshold, the cool air from outside brushing against his face. Behind him, the room returned to silence, save for the faint clatter of dishes being put away.

He stepped out without a word. Tomas stayed behind.

CHAPTER 13

Tomas Cornered

The last footsteps had faded, leaving only the hollow echo of absence. Tomas moved between the pews, stacking hymnals with slow precision. One hand on the worn covers, the other steadying the weight. Each book aligned neatly, as if order could silence the noise in his head.

The dim light through stained glass scattered muted colors across the stone floor — fractured saints watching without judgment. The scent of candle wax lingered, mixed with the dryness of old paper and something older still. A smell that clung to churches long after faith had thinned.

He adjusted a crooked cushion on the front pew. Smoothed it twice, though once was enough. His collar felt tighter than usual. Or maybe it was just the air — heavy, expectant. Outside, clouds pressed low, threatening a storm that hadn't yet earned its name.

Tomas crossed to the altar, fingertips brushing dust from the edge of the cloth. He didn't look at the cross. Instead, he checked the candles, though he knew they'd already burned out. Routine had its place — a shield against thoughts better left untouched.

At the back, a hymn book sat alone on a bench. Forgotten or left on purpose. He picked it up, thumbed through pages marked by decades of hands. The same songs, the same words. Comfort in repetition — or avoidance, depending on how one chose to see it.

The door creaked faintly behind him. He didn't turn. Not yet.

The creak of the door settled into footsteps — measured, deliberate. Tomas didn't need to look to know who it was. Cecilia's presence always arrived a moment before her voice.

"Your sermons bring such comfort in these troubled times."

The words floated, light but carrying further than they needed to. Tomas turned, hymn book still in hand. Cecilia stood near the entrance, her posture composed, eyes soft enough for an audience. Two parishioners lingered by the coat rack, slow in their gathering, ears quicker than their hands.

Tomas gave a polite nod. The kind reserved for compliments that weren't meant for him.

Cecilia stepped closer, but not too close. Just enough for her voice to carry without effort. She glanced at the altar, then back at Tomas with a smile that held no warmth — only purpose.

"It's a blessing," she continued, her tone gentle, "to have guidance that reminds us of what truly matters."

The last of the coats were taken. The shuffle of departing feet echoed against stone. Tomas placed the hymn book on the stack, aligning it carefully, giving the silence a chance to reclaim the room.

Cecilia didn't move. Her hands folded neatly in front of her, gaze steady. The door clicked shut behind the others, leaving only the weight of her words hanging in the stale air.

Tomas adjusted his sleeves, eyes avoiding hers. Praise wasn't a gift here — it was a signal.

The echo of the door latch faded, leaving a stillness that felt heavier than before. Without the audience, Cecilia's smile thinned — not gone, just stripped of its performance.

She took a step forward. The sound of her shoes on stone was soft, but deliberate. Tomas stayed where he was, fingers brushing the edge of the hymnal stack as if there was still tidying to be done.

"We must keep the community together," Cecilia said, her voice quieter now, but no less clear.

Tomas nodded once, not trusting words. His eyes followed a crack in the floor tiles, a familiar line he'd traced many times before. A map to nowhere, but it gave his gaze somewhere to rest.

Cecilia's hands smoothed the front of her coat, a gesture more about control than comfort. She let the silence stretch, knowing it spoke louder than insistence.

"Doubt can spread," she added, almost kindly. "Especially when people are vulnerable."

Her meaning wasn't hidden. It never was. Tomas shifted his weight, the collar of his shirt pressing against his throat. He looked up, meeting her eyes for a moment too long before glancing away — toward the stained glass where light no longer reached.

Cecilia followed his gaze but saw nothing there. She didn't need to. Her point had already been made.

Cecilia moved past Tomas without invitation, her fingers grazing the pulpit as she walked. A faint trace of dust clung to her fingertips — she brushed it away with a practiced swipe, eyes lingering on the wood as if it held the memory of every word ever spoken from it.

"My father drank," she said, the words falling into the still air like a statement of weather. Unemotional. Unavoidable.

Tomas remained by the pews, his hands resting at his sides now. There was nothing to tidy. Nothing left to shield him from where this was going.

"Order kept us standing." Her voice was steady, almost reflective. "Rules. Discipline. Knowing where one belonged."

She didn't look at him when she spoke. Her attention stayed on the pulpit, smoothing an invisible crease along its edge. The gesture wasn't about cleaning — it was claiming.

"Without that..." A pause. Not for effect, but because some things didn't need finishing.

Tomas watched her in silence. The faint creak of the building settling around them filled the space where words might have gone. He felt the weight of what wasn't being said — the justification, the warning, the expectation wrapped in a story of survival.

Cecilia finally turned, her expression calm, as if they'd shared nothing more than a passing thought on the weather.

Cecilia's calm gaze held him for a moment longer than necessary. Then she stepped away from the pulpit, her shoes barely making a sound against the stone floor. Tomas didn't move.

His hand found the edge of the nearest pew, fingers curling around the worn wood. The familiar texture — smooth from years of parishioners' hands — grounded him, but offered no comfort.

Cecilia adjusted her sleeve, a small nod to herself as if everything was now in its rightful place. She didn't need to say more. The shape of the conversation had already settled around him, tight and inescapable.

Tomas felt the pressure in his chest — not panic, but the slow, sinking weight of knowing. Knowing that to speak against her, against what the village wanted to believe, would be to stand alone. Not just as a priest, but as a man unwelcome in his own community.

The air felt heavier, thick with the scent of old wax and something else — the quiet suffocation of duty misused.

Cecilia's footsteps began to retreat, unhurried. She trusted him to understand what was expected. Trusted that fear, dressed as responsibility, would keep him in line.

Tomas didn't watch her leave. His grip on the pew tightened, knuckles pale against the dark wood.

The church door stood open now, Cecilia's figure framed for a moment against the dull light outside before she disappeared into the heavy air. Tomas listened to her footsteps fade, swallowed by the gravel path beyond.

His hand slipped from the pew, fingers flexing as if they no longer knew what to hold onto. The silence in the church wasn't peaceful — it pressed in from all sides, thick with the weight of decisions already made for him.

He drew a breath that didn't ease the tightness in his throat. His eyes found the pulpit, where a smear of dust still marked where Cecilia's hand had been. A small thing, but it felt larger now — a signature left behind.

Tomas lowered his head. Not in prayer. Just in quiet surrender.

"You're right, Cecilia," he said, the words barely more than air. No one to hear them but the walls that had witnessed worse.

The echo of his voice faded quickly, as if even the building was eager to forget.

He stood there a moment longer, the taste of resignation dry on his tongue. Then he moved — slow, mechanical — to close the door, shutting out the storm that hadn't yet broken.

Behind him, the church settled back into its familiar stillness. Nothing out of place. Nothing spoken of again.

CHAPTER 14

Tobbe's Outburst

The door to Napoli swung open with a faint jingle, too delicate for the weight it carried. Andreas stepped out first, one hand on the shoulder of the smaller girl, the other holding a paper bag stained with oil at the bottom corner. Elsa clung to his side, Maja trailing a half-step behind, tugging at the hem of her dress.

The sun caught the crown of his head — thinning hair slicked back, neat in a way that spoke of intention. His shirt was clean, sleeves rolled to the elbow, revealing forearms that suggested work and discipline. He glanced down at Elsa, offered a smile that didn't quite reach his eyes, then crouched to adjust Maja's sandal strap. A father, attentive and calm. The picture everyone wanted to see.

Behind him, the smell of baked dough and snus drifted from the doorway, Dilan's silhouette briefly visible before the door eased shut again. Andreas straightened, took a measured breath, and scanned the lot with the quiet assurance of a man who knew how to hold a stage without seeming to.

The girls each took a hand without being asked. They moved together toward the Volkswagen parked by the fence — faded red, washed that morning. Andreas said something low, inaudible over the distant hum of a passing car on Road 46. Elsa nodded. Maja looked up at him, then down at the gravel, kicking a loose stone.

From across the lot, an old man paused by the yellow mailbox, eyes flicking toward them before returning to his envelope. A woman with a stroller adjusted her pace, offering a polite nod as Andreas passed. He returned it with a courteous smile — nothing more, nothing less. The kind of man who handled his duties. The kind of father the village could approve of.

Tobbe leaned against the railing by the patio, a half-smoked cigarette pinched between his fingers. The sunlight caught the grease stains on his coveralls, the faded Lövgrens Maskin patch barely visible on his chest. He wasn't looking at anything in particular — until Andreas crossed his line of sight.

The cigarette paused halfway to his lips. His gaze fixed on the small figures beside Andreas. Elsa's thin arm wrapped around her father's leg. Maja stumbling to keep up, her free hand dragging the stuffed rabbit by its ear.

Tobbe's jaw tightened. He took a slow drag, held it too long. The smoke curled from his nostrils as his eyes followed the trio's path across the lot. The paper bag swung gently in Andreas' grip — a family meal, nothing out of place.

His free hand closed into a fist, knuckles whitening. The cigarette trembled between his fingers before he flicked it to the ground, grinding it under his boot with more force than needed. His breath came heavier now, shoulders rising with each exhale.

Andreas opened the car door, guiding the girls in with a patience that might've fooled anyone else. Tobbe didn't move. Didn't speak. Just watched — the weight pressing down behind his ribs, too familiar to swallow this time.

The gravel crunched under Andreas' boots as he circled to the driver's side. That was when Tobbe straightened. Hands at his sides, fists clenched tight enough to make the skin stretch pale. The warmth of the afternoon didn't reach him. All he saw was the lie playing out in front of everyone — and no one blinking.

The engine coughed to life, a low hum settling over the lot. Andreas adjusted the rearview mirror, his face reflected for a moment — calm, almost content.

Tobbe took a step forward. The sound came from deep in his chest before it reached his throat. Another step, gravel shifting under heavy boots.

"We all know what you are."

The words cut through the afternoon air, sharp and unpolished. Loud enough to turn heads at the bus stop. Loud enough to make Dilan glance up from behind the counter inside.

Andreas' hand froze on the gear stick. He didn't look over. Didn't need to. The girls sat quiet in the back seat, Elsa clutching her rabbit now, eyes fixed on the floor mat.

Tobbe stood firm, breathing hard. His voice didn't shake — it didn't need to. The weight was in the silence that followed, heavier than the words themselves. A stray breeze carried the smell of petrol and fried dough between them, but nothing moved.

A car passed on Road 46, indifferent. The moment stretched thin, the hum of Andreas' Volkswagen the only reply. A curtain twitched in the window above Pattaya. Someone watching, but no one stepping in.

Tobbe's fists slowly unclenched, fingers flexing as if the fight had already happened somewhere inside him. He didn't speak again. There was nothing else to say — not to a man like that, and not to a village that would pretend they hadn't heard.

Andreas didn't turn the key. Not yet. His hand rested on it, fingers drumming once against the steering wheel. Then he looked up — slow, deliberate — finding Tobbe in the rearview mirror.

The smirk came without effort. Barely there, but enough. The kind that wasn't meant to provoke — just to remind. A man who knew the rules of this place, and how little words like Tobbe's mattered.

Elsa shifted in her seat, her small face turned toward the window, refusing to meet her father's eyes in the mirror. Maja hummed something under her breath, a tune with no melody, fingers twisting the ear of her stuffed rabbit.

Andreas adjusted his posture, one hand casually slipping to the gear stick. His gaze lingered on Tobbe for a heartbeat longer — not a challenge, not even acknowledgment. Just quiet dismissal dressed as composure.

The Volkswagen rolled forward, tyres crunching over loose gravel, the smirk still ghosting his lips as he passed Tobbe without a glance. The sun glinted off the windshield, hiding his face as the car eased onto Road 46 and disappeared behind a bend.

Tobbe stood alone now, the echo of his own voice fading into the warm afternoon hum. No one approached. No one spoke. The village had already decided what it hadn't heard.

The afternoon light had shifted by the time Patrik pushed open the door to Napoli. The bell chimed — a dull, familiar sound — as the scent of yeast, tomato sauce, and something fried settled around him.

Dilan stood behind the counter, folding pizza boxes with the practiced rhythm of someone who'd done it a thousand times. The kitchen hummed in the background — the low whirr of the oven fan, the occasional clang of metal against metal.

Patrik stepped up, nodding a greeting. Dilan returned it without words, sliding a half-folded box aside.

"Tobbe causing a scene again," Dilan said, almost as an afterthought. His hands didn't pause, creasing cardboard with neat precision.

Patrik raised an eyebrow but didn't ask. He didn't need to. Dilan's tone told him everything — not concern, not surprise. Just routine observation, filed under village noise.

Dilan glanced up briefly, a flicker of something in his eyes — amusement, maybe. Or just the weary acknowledgment of a man who'd seen enough of Keldarp to know what passed for news.

"Outside. Earlier." He tapped the counter twice, as if that closed the matter.

Patrik let the silence sit. The smell of flour dust and warm cheese filled the gaps where questions might have been. He watched Dilan reach for another box, the conversation already drifting away like steam from the open kitchen door.

By the window, two men nursed their beers, eyes drifting between the lottery slips on the table and the street outside. One of them chuckled — low and dry.

"You know how Tobbe gets."

The other grunted in agreement, scratching at a faded tattoo on his forearm. Neither looked particularly interested. The words were more habit than conversation, like commenting on the weather or the price of petrol.

Near the counter, a woman rummaged through a rack of scratch cards, her lips pressed thin. She didn't glance up, but her head tilted slightly — enough to show she'd heard. Everyone had. No one needed the details.

Dilan slid a bottle of soda across to a teenager who handed over a crumpled note, their exchange quiet, transactional. The smell of melted cheese and snus lingered, mixing with the faint trace of gasoline that seeped in every time the door opened.

Patrik stood by the wall, waiting. Listening without leaning in. The murmur of dismissal settled over the room — the kind that smoothed rough edges, turned sharp truths into village anecdotes before they could cut too deep.

Outside, an EPA tractor rumbled past, bass rattling its loose panels. The men by the window barely noticed. Their focus returned to circling numbers on a betting slip, the world already shifting back to what made sense — horses, odds, and the comfort of looking the other way.

Patrik stepped out of Napoli, the door closing behind him with a soft click. The afternoon warmth had dulled, shadows stretching longer across the cracked asphalt.

He stood still, hands in his pockets, eyes drifting over the empty lot where the Volkswagen had been. A faint trace of exhaust still clung to the air, mixed with the lingering scent of fry oil and dust.

Across the road, the "QStar" sign above the gas station flickered weakly against the pale sky. A dog barked somewhere in the distance — sharp, then silent.

Patrik's gaze settled on the spot near the fence, where the gravel was scuffed and darkened. No sign of Tobbe now. Just quiet.

He shifted his weight, the leather of his shoes creaking softly. There was nothing to say. Nothing to fix. The village had already turned the page, as it always did.

A breeze picked up, carrying the faint rustle of leaves from the birch trees by the church. Patrik watched them move, his expression unreadable — the kind carved from years of knowing when words were useless.

He stayed there a moment longer, letting the weight settle where it belonged. Then he turned, walking away without urgency, leaving the silence to fill in what no one else would speak.

CHAPTER 15

Majvor Watches

The door opened without a sound. Just the faint click of the latch giving way.

Majvor stood there, framed by the soft light spilling from behind her. No surprise in her eyes. No need for words. She simply stepped aside, leaving space where an invitation would have been.

Patrik nodded once — more to himself than to her — and crossed the threshold. The familiar warmth of the kitchen met him, carrying with it the scent of cinnamon and something richer beneath. Cardamom, maybe. Or just memory.

Behind him, the door closed with the same quiet efficiency. The kind that didn't ask questions.

Majvor moved ahead, slippers brushing against worn linoleum. She didn't look back to check if he followed. She didn't need to.

The lace curtains filtered the grey afternoon into something softer. The ticking of the wall clock marked time that didn't press here. On the counter, a bowl of dough rested under a clean cloth — rising slowly, without urgency.

Patrik shrugged off his jacket, hanging it on the same hook he always used. The one that had held his father's coat, years ago. Some things didn't change. Some things couldn't.

Majvor was already at the stove, her hand reaching for the coffee pot without asking. Without expectation.

Patrik sat down at the kitchen table. His chair. The wood creaked under his weight — a familiar sound in a room that didn't require conversation to feel occupied.

The cup was placed in front of him without ceremony. Faded porcelain, a small chip on the handle — the same cup as always.

Majvor poured her own and sat opposite him. The steam rose between them, carrying the scent of strong, black coffee. No milk. No sugar. Just as it was meant to be.

The kitchen held its warmth, but outside the grey pressed against the windows. The lace curtains softened it, but didn't keep it out. A breeze stirred the fabric now and then — a reminder that the world beyond hadn't changed.

Patrik wrapped his hands around the cup, letting the heat settle into his fingers. The first sip was too hot, but he didn't flinch. It wasn't about the taste.

Majvor's gaze drifted to the window, watching nothing in particular. The wall clock ticked steadily behind her, marking time that neither of them needed to acknowledge.

The smell of baking lingered — cinnamon, cardamom, and yeast still rising beneath the cloth on the counter. A quiet promise that didn't ask for attention.

They sat like that. No words. No need for them. The coffee did what words couldn't — filled the space, anchored them both.

Patrik let his shoulders drop, just enough to notice. Majvor didn't. She didn't need to.

Majvor rose without a word, collecting the empty cups with steady hands. The faint clink of porcelain was the only sound as she set them by the sink.

Patrik stayed seated, his eyes following the slow, familiar movements. She lifted the cloth from the bowl, revealing the pale dome of dough beneath. It had risen well — as it always did.

She dusted the counter with flour, the fine powder catching in the afternoon light. Then, with sleeves pushed back, she turned the dough out and began to knead. Rhythmic. Patient. Each fold and press carrying the weight of years spent doing the same thing, for the same reasons.

The soft thud of hands against dough filled the room, blending with the ticking clock. Patrik watched her work — not because there was anything remarkable in it, but because there was nothing remarkable in it.

Now and then, Majvor glanced his way. Not to check on him. Just to let him know she knew he was still there.

Outside, a gust of wind pushed harder against the windowpane, rattling it in its frame. Majvor didn't react. The dough needed her attention more than the weather did.

Patrik leaned back slightly, the chair legs creaking against the floor. His hands rested on his thighs, empty now that the coffee was gone.

The silence stretched — not heavy, not light. Just there. Like the flour dusting the air, settling unnoticed.

Majvor brushed the last of the flour from her hands, the motion slow and deliberate. She stood for a moment, looking at the neat ball of dough resting on the counter. Covered it again with the cloth. Let it rise a little longer.

Patrik hadn't moved. His gaze was fixed somewhere between the window and the past.

Majvor wiped her palms on her apron, then leaned against the counter. Her eyes found him — steady, knowing, without expectation.

The clock ticked on. The wind outside had quieted, leaving only the faint creak of the old house settling into itself.

When she spoke, it was almost as if she hadn't. The words landed gently, but didn't soften anything.

"He's the only one saying it out loud."

She didn't look away when she said it. Didn't soften it with a smile or follow it with anything else. Just left it there — the only truth worth offering.

Patrik's jaw tightened, barely. His eyes dropped to the table, tracing the grain of the wood with a focus that had nothing to do with the surface.

Majvor pushed herself off the counter and turned back to her work. The cloth shifted slightly as she adjusted it over the dough, hands as steady as her voice had been.

Nothing more needed saying.

The coffee had long since cooled, but Patrik lifted the cup anyway. The last sip was bitter, the way it always was when left too long. He swallowed it without reaction.

Majvor didn't turn from the counter. She was shaping the dough now, her movements unhurried. The kind of work that filled the space where conversation didn't belong.

Patrik set the cup down gently. The hollow sound of porcelain against wood marked the end of whatever this had been — not a conversation, not a visit. Just necessary.

He stood, his chair scraping softly against the floor. Reached for his jacket, still hanging where he'd left it. The fabric felt colder than when he'd arrived.

Majvor glanced over her shoulder, just once. A brief acknowledgment — not a farewell.

Patrik nodded. A small gesture, but enough. He didn't thank her. That wasn't what this was for.

The weight in his chest hadn't lifted, but it had settled — like something packed tighter, easier to carry for a while longer.

He moved to the door, his footsteps absorbed by the worn rug. His hand found the handle, pausing only for the briefest moment before pushing it open.

The cool air met him as he stepped outside. The door closed behind him without a sound.

Through the window, Majvor watched Patrik cross the small patch of gravel, his shoulders squared against the chill. The sky hung low, heavy with the kind of grey that didn't need to deliver rain to make its point.

He didn't look back. He never did. That wasn't his way — and she wouldn't have expected it.

The curtain settled as she let it fall back into place. The kitchen felt no different for his absence. The same warmth, the same ticking clock. The same dough waiting under her hands.

Majvor turned back to the counter. The rolls were shaped now, lined up in even rows on the baking sheet. She brushed them lightly with egg, each stroke measured and precise.

Outside, the wind stirred again, but the walls held steady. They always had.

She slid the tray into the oven, the quiet click of the door sealing it shut. A scent would fill the room soon enough — something sweet to mask the bitter air that clung to anyone who stepped beyond her threshold.

Majvor wiped her hands on the apron, then paused. For a moment, she stood still, listening to nothing in particular.

Then she moved on. The dough wouldn't wait, and in Keldarp, survival was knowing which silences to leave untouched.

CHAPTER 16

The decision is made

The door clicked shut behind him with the same sound it made every morning. Andreas didn't lock it — no need in a place like this. The gravel beneath his boots shifted as he walked the short path to the roadside.

The air smelled of cut grass. Someone further down had been out early with the mower. A breeze caught the edge of his T-shirt, cool against skin still warm from sleep. The sky was clear. It would be a good day, by most measures.

He reached the mailbox, its red paint faded and chipped along the edges. The lid stuck for a moment before giving way with a metallic scrape. Inside — the usual clutter. A rolled-up flyer promising discounts on grill meat, a thin envelope from the electricity company, something glossy from a bank he didn't use.

And then the white one. The kind that didn't need color to demand attention. Windowed, stamped with the municipality's emblem — a gold crown and the letter U, surrounded by small trefoils on a blue shield — sterile and precise. He slid it out with two fingers, the paper stiff against his skin.

No change in his face. No pause.

He stacked it beneath the others, pinning it in place with his thumb. The lid clattered shut. A bird called somewhere in the trees, sharp and indifferent.

Andreas turned back toward the house, the envelopes held loosely at his side. The gravel shifted again, same as it did every morning.

He didn't make it to the door.

The breeze caught the edge of the top envelope, fluttering it against his thumb. Andreas stopped at the step, the morning sun casting his shadow long across the porch boards. The wood was starting to grey — something to deal with before autumn.

He shifted the stack, pulling the white envelope free. The others slipped under his arm without care. His thumb traced the glued edge, feeling the slight ridge beneath the paper's smooth surface. No hesitation. Just routine.

The tear was clean, practiced. The sound barely rose above the distant hum of a lawnmower starting up again.

He unfolded the letter where he stood, the sunlight catching on the sterile black print. The paper smelled faintly of toner and recycled pulp — the scent of decisions made elsewhere.

His eyes moved, but not with urgency. He already knew where to look. The middle of the page. That's where verdicts lived. Everything else was padding — dates, reference numbers, polite constructions pretending to soften the blow that never came.

A fly landed on his forearm. He didn't brush it away.

The wind shifted. The grass beyond the ditch swayed, indifferent.

The letters blurred into blocks of ink, but his gaze found the sentence without effort. It was where they always put it — after the formalities, before the disclaimers.

"…the decision has been made to grant continued custody to Mr. Andreas Karlsson, in the interest of providing stability for the children."

His eyes rested on the word — stability. As if it meant something.

The paper shifted slightly in his hand as the breeze passed through again. The edge lifted, then settled. He didn't move.

A crow called from somewhere beyond the trees. Sharp. Out of place against the softness of the morning.

The letter weighed nothing, but it anchored him there on the step. Bare feet would have felt the coolness of the wood, but his boots dulled it. Just as the words dulled everything else.

The hum of the lawnmower faded, replaced by the faint sound of a car passing on the distant road. Life continuing. Decisions delivered.

Andreas let his eyes linger a moment longer, though there was nothing more to see. The rest of the page was noise — explanations no one would read, justifications no one would question.

He folded the paper once, his thumb pressing along the crease with quiet precision.

The fold stopped short of the bottom edge. His thumb held it open, eyes dropping to the final paragraph.

Standard text. Rights to appeal. Deadlines, contact details, polite invitations to contest what no one ever overturned.

The font was smaller here. As if they knew no one cared to read this far. A gesture, nothing more — like holding a door open that led nowhere.

Andreas let the paper sag in his hand. The breeze caught at the loose corner, but he tightened his grip, crinkling the edge slightly.

Somewhere inside the house, a faint thud — a toy dropped, or footsteps too light to matter. He didn't look back.

The crow called again, further away now. The hum of the village settling into its day. Birds, engines, distant voices carried by the wind. All of it indifferent.

His eyes traced the last line once more, not reading, just marking the end of it. A number to call. An address to write to. If someone felt inclined.

He didn't.

The letter closed with the same ease it had opened, the crease sharper this time beneath his fingers.

Andreas slid the letter back into its envelope, the paper gliding along the edges with practiced ease. The flap hung open, but he didn't bother sealing it. There was no need.

The other envelopes were still tucked under his arm — bills, offers, noise. He placed them on top, the official white disappearing beneath overdue reminders and supermarket discounts.

He turned without looking at the road or the sky. The door stood where it always did, paint peeling at the frame, handle worn smooth by years of the same grip.

The hinges gave a soft creak as he stepped inside. The coolness of the hallway wrapped around him — familiar, still.

He set the stack on the narrow table by the door. The envelopes fanned slightly, the official one indistinguishable now among the rest.

From deeper in the house, a small voice called out. Not words — just the sound of waiting.

Andreas closed the door with a quiet click. No glance back, no second thought.

The letter had done its job. The rest was already his.

CHAPTER 17

Small Bruises

The sleeve slipped as she reached for her father's hand. Just a second — enough.

Patrik saw the bruise. Small. Dull yellow at the edges, fading toward green. Not fresh. Not accidental. It sat low on Maja's forearm like something placed there on purpose.

Andreas didn't notice. Or didn't care. His grip on her wrist was casual, practiced. Not tight — just there.

Elsa walked ahead, silent, hands in her jacket pockets. Patrik couldn't see her face. The girls said nothing. Neither did their father. The three of them passed like any other family walking through a quiet village street in early autumn — too quiet, if you listened properly.

The air was still. No birds. No wind. Just the sound of boots on wet gravel and the creak of Andreas's old leather jacket as he moved.

They didn't acknowledge Patrik. He didn't call out. Just watched.

The air smelled of wet asphalt and something faintly sour — the way Keldarp did when the clouds pressed low and the earth refused to dry. Patrik stood still, letting them pass, offering a nod that Andreas barely returned. No words. None needed.

Maja's sleeve fell back into place as they walked on. Small boots tapping against the uneven pavement, too light to leave a mark. Patrik watched until they turned the corner by Jönssons Livs — the boarded-up windows of the closed down grocery store swallowing them like always.

Patrik stood still after they disappeared. A moment longer than necessary. Then he turned back the way he'd come, footsteps soft against the damp gravel. No hurry. No sound but his own boots and the low hum of something distant — maybe a mower, maybe just the village breathing.

The bruise stayed with him. Not sharp. Not loud. Just a quiet stain at the edge of his mind, refusing to be explained away.

His car was parked by the spring. He unlocked it without looking around and slid behind the wheel. The seat was still warm from the sun, though the sky had gone flat. He sat there a while before starting the engine.

The road out of Keldarp was empty. Trees pressed in close, already losing their leaves. He drove in silence.

The office smelled of old coffee and the faint heat of machines left running too long. Fluorescents buzzed overhead. Patrik sat at his desk, the cursor blinking against a white screen that had nothing urgent to say.

He typed slowly. Maja Karlsson. Approximate age: two. Minor discoloration observed on left forearm. Possible contusion. No obvious external cause.

He paused. Let the words settle. Then added — routine observation during incidental encounter. No further action required at this time.

He clicked save. The sound was soft, swallowed by the drone of the office. Nothing in the room acknowledged it. Not even him.

Outside, the sky hung low over the asphalt, the kind of weather that muted everything — including doubt.

Elin's chair creaked as she settled in across from him, coffee cup in hand. The lid wasn't on straight — a thin line of dark liquid traced down her thumb. She didn't notice, or didn't care.

Patrik kept his eyes on the monitor, the case file still open. The bruise — reduced to a line of text — sat there, waiting for a reaction that wouldn't come.

"Anything serious?" Elin's voice was casual, words stretched by routine more than curiosity.

Patrik shrugged. "Not really."

She glanced at the screen, took a sip. The coffee stain deepened on her skin. "Kids play rough."

The hum of the copier filled the pause. Outside the window, the sky pressed low — a uniform grey that made it hard to tell if it was noon or evening. Patrik nodded once, the way you did when there was nothing left to add.

Elin leaned back, the chair protesting again. Another sip, another shrug. Her gaze drifted to her own screen, already moving on.

The office returned to its rhythm

The coffee smell lingered after Elin left, faint and bitter. Patrik stayed where he was, eyes fixed on the screen, though the words had blurred into nothing.

The cursor blinked in quiet impatience.

He heard Elin's voice again from across the office — light, indifferent, already absorbed in something else. The rhythm of normalcy was hard to break in a place built for routine.

His hand moved, slow and deliberate, closing the file with a few muted clicks. The report folded into the system, just another note among hundreds. Documented. Filed. Forgotten.

Elin glanced over, catching his movement. She raised her cup slightly, a half gesture of closure. "Yeah... probably," Patrik said, the words low, almost automatic.

She nodded without looking up again.

Patrik's gaze returned to the dark screen, his reflection faint in the glass. The office hum filled the space where doubt sat heavier than anything typed.

Outside, the grey pressed against the windows, the kind of weather that made everything look the same — clean, dull, easy to ignore.

He leaned back, letting the chair creak beneath him. The weight wasn't in the file. It never was.

CHAPTER 18

The Note Revealed

The grey light through the station windows didn't change. It pressed against the glass, dull and heavy, like it had been there for years. Patrik sat at his desk, the case file open in front of him. Pages spread out, edges slightly curled. His fingers tapped the wood — steady, without rhythm. Not impatience. Just something to fill the silence.

Across the room, Sebbe typed. Quiet keystrokes, deliberate. No conversation. No need.

The air smelled of something reheated. Probably from the break room. It mixed with the faint trace of dust and old paper. Patrik shifted in his chair, eyes fixed on the note lying atop the file. It wasn't out of place. It wasn't screaming for attention. But it sat there — too neat, too clean.

He rubbed his thumb along the edge of a report, but his gaze stayed on the signature at the bottom of the note. Sofia's name. Written like it always was. Except it wasn't. He didn't know how he knew — he just did.

His fingers stopped tapping. The weight in his chest hadn't moved since morning. Sebbe didn't look up. The station hummed with fluorescent light, steady and indifferent.

"Not nothing." The words weren't spoken, but they echoed all the same.

Patrik's hand moved without decision, drawing the note closer. The crisp paper made a faint sound against the rougher reports beneath it — too clean, like it didn't belong in a file that had already gathered the weight of failure.

He leaned forward, elbows on the desk. The signature caught the light differently than the rest of the text. His finger traced along the curve of the "S," stopping where the ink line met the paper too sharply. No bleed. No hesitation. Perfect in a way handwriting never was.

Behind him, Sebbe's typing slowed. Not enough to notice unless you were listening for it. Patrik didn't turn.

The note was short. Practical. The kind of thing a mother in a hurry might write — except she hadn't. He could see it now, in the way the letters held no life. A message stripped of human touch.

His thumb hovered over the corner of the page, as if the pressure alone could reveal what was already obvious. It wasn't proof. It never was. But it was there — plain as day for anyone willing to look past convenience.

Outside the window, the grey held steady. No movement. No sign that the world cared whether ink was real or pasted.

Patrik let the note rest on the desk, its edges perfectly aligned with the case file beneath. He reached for the phone, the handset cold against his palm. The number to forensics was already worn into his memory — a small efficiency that didn't matter now.

Two rings. Then a voice. Flat, distracted.

"Ulricehamn, Patrik Bockgren." His voice was steady, stripped of anything that might sound like urgency.

The explanation was brief. The note. The signature. Something off. He kept it clinical — facts only. There was a pause on the other end, the kind that told him they were already moving on in their mind.

"People paste in signatures all the time," the voice said. "Could be nothing."

Patrik's pen, held between his fingers, stayed still over the notepad. No notes to take.

"Send it in if you want," the voice added, the words softened by indifference. "We'll look at it when we have time."

The line didn't go dead, but it might as well have. Patrik gave a quiet acknowledgment — not agreement, just receipt — and lowered the handset back into its cradle. The click of plastic against plastic was the only reply the call deserved.

The pen remained idle in his hand. Outside, the sky pressed heavier against the windows, as if waiting for him to realize what he already knew.

The phone sat where he left it. Still. Useless.

Patrik leaned back, eyes fixed on the note. It hadn't changed. Same clean lines, same lie printed neat enough to pass as truth.

He reached out, not to touch it, just to let his hand hover above the paper. There was nothing left to feel. The call had confirmed that much.

In the corner of the office, the hum of a printer started up — someone else's task moving forward. Routine carried on, indifferent to doubt.

Patrik's gaze didn't waver. The signature stared back, quiet and certain. He knew what it was. Knew what it meant. But knowing wasn't enough. Not here. Not with this.

The stale air pressed in, heavy with the smell of old coffee and something reheated long ago. He didn't notice when his hand dropped back to the desk, fingers brushing against the edge of the file.

There was no anger. No frustration. Just the familiar weight settling deeper — the kind that came when the truth found no purchase.

He stayed like that, watching the note as if it might eventually confess. It didn't.

The file shut with a soft thud, but Sebbe didn't react. His eyes stayed on the screen, fingers moving steadily over the keyboard. Forms, reports — the kind of paperwork that filled days without leaving a mark.

Patrik watched him. The set of his shoulders, the way his jaw tightened just slightly with each line typed. No questions. No glances across the desk like he used to — back when he still believed every detail mattered.

The fluorescent lights cast a pale sheen over Sebbe's hair, making him look younger and older at the same time. The weight hadn't come all at once. It had settled in, quiet and patient, like everything else in this job.

A printer somewhere in the office whirred to life, then stopped. The smell of stale coffee drifted in from the corridor. Sebbe kept typing, his face unreadable — not out of control, but because there was nothing left to say.

Patrik leaned back, letting the silence stretch between them. This wasn't defiance. It wasn't even disappointment. It was just survival — knowing when to stop pushing against a wall that wouldn't move.

Outside, the grey sky pressed down. Inside, Sebbe filed the future away, one keystroke at a time.

CHAPTER 19

Tomas' Confession

The gravel shifted under Tomas' shoes as he reached the porch. The faint wind carried the scent of cooling earth and distant woodsmoke. He didn't knock.

The door opened before his hand could rise. Majvor stood there, framed by the dim light behind her. No words. Just a look that said she'd been expecting him — though neither of them had arranged this.

Tomas nodded, more to himself than to her. His cap remained in his hand, fingers pressing the worn brim. The kind of gesture a man makes when there's nothing left to prepare for.

Majvor stepped aside, slow and deliberate. The space she left was enough. He crossed the threshold without thanks, without greeting. The floorboards creaked beneath his weight — a familiar sound that didn't soften his steps.

Behind him, the door closed with a quiet finality. The kind that didn't need a lock.

In the kitchen, the light was low — a single bulb casting long shadows across the table. Two cups sat waiting. Steam long gone.

The clock on the wall marked the seconds with indifferent ticks, each one louder than necessary.

Tomas placed his cap on the edge of the counter, careful, as if noise might betray something they both already knew. He didn't sit. Not yet.

Majvor watched him with the patience of someone who understood that some arrivals take longer than the distance walked.

Tomas sat down without being asked. The chair gave a soft groan beneath him — the only sound between them. Majvor followed, her movements unhurried, settling into the seat opposite.

The table stretched between them, marked by years of use — faint scratches, a ring where a hot pot once stood too long. Between them, the two coffee cups. Still full. Still untouched.

The dim light above cast their shadows onto the surface, long and distorted. Tomas kept his eyes on the cup in front of him, fingers resting on the rim without lifting it. The coffee had gone cold, but neither of them reached for it.

Outside, the wind brushed against the windowpane — a faint, irregular rhythm that didn't ask for attention but filled the gaps where words might have been.

The clock ticked on. A steady reminder that time was moving, even if they weren't.

Majvor's gaze held steady, not probing, not offering. Just there. A presence across the worn wood, patient in a way that made speaking harder, not easier.

Tomas shifted in his seat, the fabric of his trousers whispering against the chair. His shoulders squared, then sank again — the motion of a man rehearsing something he'd already decided not to say. Not yet.

The cups remained where they were. The space between them spoke louder than either of them could manage.

Tomas' fingers traced the edge of the cup, round and round, until even that small movement felt too loud. He pulled his hand back, resting it flat on the table. The other followed — palms down, as if steadying himself against something unseen.

His eyes dropped to his hands. The skin across his knuckles was dry, a faint crack along the thumb where he'd split it stacking chairs after service. He pressed the thumb against his forefinger, watching the white line bloom, then fade.

The first breath he took wasn't meant for speaking. But the second carried words, brittle and low.

"I thought…"

The sentence hung there, unfinished. Tomas swallowed, his gaze fixed on the hands that had performed a hundred blessings, folded in prayer more times than he could count — but never shook when they should have.

"It wasn't doubt," he said, voice barely more than a whisper. "It was knowing. And choosing to look away."

The clock answered him with another tick. The wind outside shifted, a loose branch tapping once against the glass before falling quiet again.

He didn't lift his head. The weight of Majvor's presence was enough — steady, unflinching.

"I told myself it was for the sake of peace," Tomas continued, the words slower now, each one pulled from a place he'd kept locked. "For the village."

His shoulders tensed, then sagged — composure giving way under the truth he could no longer keep contained.

"But it wasn't peace," he said, almost to himself. "It was fear."

Tomas' hands slipped from the table to his lap, fingers curling into fists before loosening again. His head bowed lower, as if the weight of his words had finally settled on his neck.

"I knew..."

The words came out thin, frayed at the edges. He let them hang there, no rush to finish what didn't need explaining.

The chair beneath him creaked as his shoulders slumped forward, the collar of his shirt pulling tight around his neck — a reminder of the role he wore too well, for too long.

"I knew what he was. What he did." His voice cracked, but not from emotion — from exhaustion. "And I stayed quiet."

The wind rattled faintly against the window again, but neither of them looked up. The kitchen felt smaller now, the walls pressing in with the truth laid bare between them.

Tomas dragged a hand over his face, stopping at his mouth, as if holding back more words that served no purpose. His breath warmed his palm before he let it fall away.

"Not faith. Not duty," he said, the bitterness flat and dull. "Just cowardice."

He didn't search Majvor's face for forgiveness. He already knew it wasn't there — not because she lacked kindness, but because some things weren't hers to give.

The clock kept ticking, indifferent. The coffee remained untouched, cold as the silence that followed.

Tomas' words faded into the stillness, leaving only the faint hum of the refrigerator and the relentless ticking of the clock. He kept his gaze fixed on the table, as if meeting her eyes would make the weight of it all unbearable.

Majvor didn't move. Her hands rested calmly in her lap, her back straight against the chair. She watched him — not with pity, not with reproach — just the steady gaze of someone who had long understood that some burdens weren't meant to be shared, only spoken aloud.

The wind outside had settled. In its absence, the silence deepened, pressing against the thin walls of the kitchen. The kind of silence that didn't ask for words, because there were none that would make a difference.

Tomas shifted, sensing the space she left untouched. No hand reaching out. No soft words to ease what couldn't be eased.

Majvor's eyes held his shame without flinching, like a mirror that refused to blur the reflection. She offered no nod, no gesture of understanding — just presence. The kind that neither condemned nor forgave.

The coffee cups stood between them, cooling reminders that some rituals weren't meant for comfort tonight.

Tomas let out a breath he hadn't noticed holding, but it didn't lighten him. It only settled the truth more firmly on his shoulders.

The silence stretched, dense and unmoving. Tomas' breathing had settled into something shallow, as if drawing too much air might stir what should stay still.

Majvor's gaze didn't waver. She let the quiet do its work — let it press into the spaces where excuses usually lived.

When she finally spoke, her voice was low, steady. No judgment. No softness either.

"We all carry what we choose not to say."

The words landed without ceremony. A simple fact, laid bare between them like another object on the table — heavier than the cups, colder than the room.

Tomas didn't respond. His eyes stayed down, fixed on the grain of the wood as if searching for a way through it.

Majvor didn't offer more. She leaned back slightly, hands folding over each other — not dismissing him, but marking that nothing else needed to be said.

The clock ticked on, indifferent to confessions or truths. Outside, the wind had died completely, leaving the faint creak of the house settling in its place.

Tomas' jaw tightened, but he gave no sign of protest. The line wasn't meant to provoke. It was simply the shape of things as they were.

In the stillness that followed, even the unsaid felt accounted for.

Tomas pushed back his chair, the legs scraping softly against the floor. He reached for his cap without looking at Majvor, fingers lingering on the worn fabric as if expecting it to offer some steadiness.

He stood, shoulders hunched—not from age, but from the shape the truth had carved into him tonight.

Majvor didn't rise. She watched as he moved to the door, each step measured, like a man walking through water.

At the threshold, Tomas paused. His hand hovered over the latch, but he didn't turn back. Whatever had passed between them was done.

The door opened with a quiet groan, letting in the cool night air. The faint scent of damp earth and something distant — woodsmoke, perhaps — met him as he stepped outside.

The wind had dropped, leaving the village wrapped in stillness. No lights in the windows. Just darkness and the soft crunch of gravel underfoot as Tomas walked away, his frame folding in on itself against the empty road ahead.

Behind him, Majvor rose without haste. She gathered the untouched cups, their contents long cold, and carried them to the sink.

Water ran. The clock kept ticking. No words followed.

CHAPTER 20

Cecilia's Final Justification

The gravel crunched softly under Patrik's boots as he stood by the trimmed lilac bushes. The sun was warm on his back, casting his shadow long across the path. Birds sang somewhere out of sight — a bright, careless tune that didn't belong here.

Cecilia's footsteps were quieter. Sensible shoes on well-kept grass. When she appeared, it was as if she had always been part of the garden — neat, composed, exactly where she should be.

Her smile arrived before her words. Serene. Pleased. The kind of smile people wore when they believed things were as they ought to be.

"Patrik."

She said it like a neighbor commenting on the weather. No weight. No history.

He nodded once, eyes following a bird as it darted between branches. The scent of lilacs thickened in the still air.

"A beautiful morning," she added, folding her hands lightly in front of her. Her posture was relaxed — the calm of someone convinced the storm had passed.

Patrik let the silence stretch. There was nothing to agree with. The sun didn't care what had been buried.

Cecilia didn't seem to notice. Her gaze swept over the garden, lingering on nothing, as if admiring her own handiwork.

"It's good to see things settling again." The words came with a gentle breath, almost like a prayer.

Another nod from Patrik. The gravel shifted under his boot as he adjusted his stance, the shadow of him cutting across the path like a crack in the calm.

Cecilia's smile held. She didn't look at him — not really. Her eyes were on the church beyond, where the white walls gleamed against the blue sky. As if they were both standing in the aftermath of a summer rain, rather than in the ruins no one would name.

Cecilia's gaze drifted back from the church, settling on Patrik as if remembering he was there. Her hands, still clasped, gave a small, contented squeeze — like she was holding something precious and fragile.

"What matters now," she said, her voice soft enough to blend with the birdsong, "is unity. Not blame."

The words hung in the air, sweet as the lilacs, just as heavy.

Patrik watched a breeze stir the grass at their feet. The movement was gentle, almost careful — as if nature itself respected the quiet fiction being woven here.

Cecilia took a step closer, her shoes silent on the trimmed lawn. She tilted her head, the smile never leaving her face. "People need to heal. Together."

Her tone was the same one used at funerals, at parish halls over dry cake — the practiced comfort that asked nothing and offered less.

Patrik's eyes dropped to her hands. The way her fingers intertwined, knuckles pale with restraint, told him more than her words. There was no tremor, no hesitation. Only certainty.

Above them, a blackbird called out — clear and bright, cutting through the softness like a reminder that life continued, indifferent.

Cecilia followed the sound with a faint nod, as if it confirmed her point. "Keldarp has been through enough," she murmured. "It's time we look forward."

Patrik didn't answer. The gravel under his heel shifted again, a quiet response neither of them acknowledged.

The sun warmed the back of his neck. The scent of grass and lilac thickened, wrapping the garden in a calm that felt too deliberate. Too easy.

Cecilia's smile deepened — pleased with the silence. It was agreement, as far as she was concerned.

Cecilia's hands loosened, fingers brushing imaginary dust from her skirt. Her gaze drifted past Patrik, settling somewhere beyond the garden — where the village lay out of sight but never out of mind.

"Of course..." Her voice softened further, almost tender. "If only Sofia had fulfilled her duties..."

The words came out like a sigh, wrapped in sorrow too practiced to be real.

Patrik's jaw tightened, but he didn't move. The shadow he cast stretched between them, untouched by the sunlit ease in her tone.

Cecilia shook her head, slow and deliberate. Her lips pressed together in a mimicry of grief — the kind that asked for no answers because it had already decided them.

"It's such a shame," she continued, eyes glistening with nothing but self-assurance. "The children... they deserved better."

The breeze caught a strand of her hair, lifting it before letting it fall neatly back into place. She didn't notice. Her focus remained fixed on that imagined horizon where all blame could be neatly folded away with the absent mother.

"Andreas is doing what he can," she added, voice low, as if confiding a painful truth. "No one can say he doesn't try."

Patrik let his gaze fall to the gravel, where small weeds pushed through the cracks — persistent, unwelcome, ignored until they became part of the path.

Cecilia's head tilted, a gesture of sorrow so well-rehearsed it bordered on graceful. "We must remember that."

The birds kept singing. The sun kept shining. And beneath Cecilia's gentle words, the knife twisted — so delicately she'd never feel the blood on her hands.

Cecilia's words drifted on without pause, as if the weight of them hadn't just settled between them. She turned slightly, her eyes following a butterfly that flitted over the lilacs — delicate, aimless.

"But now we have peace," she said, almost to herself. "The girls are where they belong. The community can breathe again."

Her hands moved as she spoke, smoothing invisible creases along her sleeve. The same hands that had clasped in unity moments before, now gestured with quiet authority — stitching together judgment and consolation without noticing the thread.

"It's important we don't dwell on past mistakes," she continued, her voice light, almost cheerful. "Especially when some choices... led us here."

Patrik watched her, expression blank. The sun caught in her glasses, hiding her eyes behind a sheen of reflected sky.

"Forgiveness," she said, with a small nod, as if concluding a sermon no one had asked for. "That's what holds a place like this together."

The scent of freshly cut grass mixed with the fading lilacs, a sweetness that clung too long. Cecilia stepped along the garden path, her shoes barely disturbing the gravel — her words flowing easily between unity and quiet condemnation, as if they were the same thing.

"Andreas understood that," she added, her tone warm with approval. "He took responsibility, even when others faltered."

Patrik's shadow shifted as the sun climbed higher, stretching thin across the stones. He didn't speak. There was no need — Cecilia was too busy weaving her version of peace, blind to the knots of blame tangled in every sentence.

She smiled again, pleased with the picture she'd painted, unaware that the cracks beneath it were already showing.

Cecilia's voice faded, her monologue complete. She stood with her hands folded again, eyes on the church walls gleaming in the sun — a picture of quiet satisfaction.

Patrik didn't move. His gaze held on her, steady and unreadable. The long shadow at his feet stretched toward her but never touched.

The breeze had died. The birds sang on, indifferent to the weight pressing down on the garden. The scent of lilacs felt heavier now, too sweet, like something left too long in the sun.

Cecilia glanced at him, expecting — what, exactly? Agreement? Gratitude? A shared understanding that never existed.

Patrik offered nothing. No nod. No polite murmur. Just the kind of silence that couldn't be mistaken for peace.

His hands stayed loose at his sides, fingers brushing against the seam of his trousers — a small, grounding gesture. The gravel beneath his boots remained still. He let the quiet stretch, knowing she'd fill it with whatever she needed to hear.

Cecilia shifted her weight, her smile flickering but holding firm. She looked past him now, toward the path leading back to the church entrance. The conversation, if it could be called that, was over.

Patrik's eyes followed a crack running through the stone border of the flower bed. Small weeds pushed through, stubborn and ignored — like truths no one wanted to pull out by the root.

He stayed silent. Not out of respect. Not out of defeat. But because some things, once buried, only rot deeper when spoken aloud.

Cecilia gave a small, approving nod — to herself more than to Patrik. The kind of gesture reserved for tasks completed, order restored.

"Take care, Patrik."

Her voice was light, almost warm. As if they'd shared nothing more than a pleasant exchange beneath the summer sun.

She turned without waiting for a response, her steps measured along the gravel path. Each footfall quiet, rehearsed — the walk of someone confident that everything was in its rightful place.

The hem of her skirt brushed against the trimmed grass. Her figure grew smaller as she moved toward the church, framed by white walls and weathered gravestones. The spire reached into the clear sky, pristine against a backdrop that didn't care what was buried beneath it.

Patrik watched her go. His shadow stretched long and thin across the garden, a dark line that didn't follow her.

Cecilia paused at the church door, adjusting her glasses, then disappeared inside without a glance back.

The birds kept singing. The scent of lilacs lingered, too sweet in the stillness she left behind.

Patrik remained where he stood, the sun warm on his shoulders, knowing that beneath the calm surface, truth and decency had been sealed away — just another thing Keldarp chose not to speak of.

CHAPTER 21

Flowers in Their Hair

The maypole stood where it always did. Fresh birch leaves wrapped tight around the pole, flowers woven into uneven crowns. Children ran circles around it, their laughter sharp against the hum of folk music from a portable speaker balanced on a folding table.

Sunlight caught on plastic cups and paper plates. The scent of grilled sausage drifted across the green, mixing with spilled beer and trampled grass. Someone had set up a makeshift game of kubb, the wooden blocks already stained from years of use. A group of men watched, half-interested, bottles hanging loose in their hands.

Patrik moved through it without purpose. A nod here. A murmur there. Faces greeted him with the same smiles they offered everyone else — wide, practiced, a little too bright. No one mentioned Sofia. No one asked questions that didn't have easy answers.

Cecilia's voice rose above the crowd for a moment — a reminder about the next song, a call for more dancers. It was met with cheerful compliance. Tradition didn't require thought. Just movement. Just noise.

A little girl stumbled near Patrik's feet, her flower crown slipping over one ear. She giggled, scrambled up, and ran back to the others. Her knees were grass-stained. No one noticed. Or pretended not to.

The sky was a postcard blue. The kind of day people wished for when they thought of Midsummer. Perfect, if you didn't look too closely. If you kept your eyes on the games, the food, the dance steps passed down without question.

Patrik glanced at the maypole again. Birch leaves rustled where they'd been wrapped, a few flower petals catching the breeze. Around it, Keldarp danced — as if nothing had ever happened.

The laughter around the maypole softened as heads turned. Not all at once — just a ripple, like wind through tall grass. Andreas Karlsson walked across the green, a daughter holding each hand.

Elsa and Maja wore matching white dresses. Too formal for the games, too clean for the grass. Long sleeves despite the warmth. Their flower crowns sat neatly, not a petal out of place. Small feet moved carefully, as if they knew falling wasn't an option today.

Andreas smiled. The kind that didn't reach his eyes but passed for genuine if you weren't looking. He nodded to familiar faces, exchanged quiet greetings. A clap on his shoulder from one of the men by the grill. A murmured "Good to see you out." No one mentioned the sleeves. No one looked too long.

The girls stood close to him when he paused. Elsa's fingers tightened around his. Maja kept her gaze on the grass, the toe of her shoe tracing invisible lines in the dirt. A woman crouched to offer them candy from a paper bag — bright wrappers, the universal language of festivals. They each took one, polite, mechanical.

Andreas ruffled Elsa's hair, careful not to disturb the crown. His voice was low, but the words didn't matter. It was the performance that counted. A father bringing his daughters to celebrate — just like any other family.

Patrik watched from where he stood, unseen in the shifting crowd. The polite nods. The smiles that held too long. The way the village welcomed him back into the fold without a single question asked.

The speaker crackled as the next song began. Andreas guided the girls forward, their small hands still locked in his. The white sleeves fluttered as they moved — thin fabric hiding everything no one wanted to see.

Cecilia's voice rose above the music, clear and practiced. She stood near the maypole, clipboard in hand, the sun catching the silver strands in her neatly pinned hair. A flower crown rested on her head, perfectly symmetrical.

"Let's enjoy this beautiful day!"

The words floated over the crowd, met with scattered applause and a few cheers. Children gathered at her feet, waiting for instructions. Parents lingered behind, grateful for someone else to take charge.

Cecilia moved with purpose, pointing out who would lead the next dance, where the line for the grill should form, reminding the teenagers to keep the soda crates in order. Every detail smoothed over before it had a chance to wrinkle.

She laughed at the right moments — light, controlled. A hand on a shoulder here, a gentle correction there. No one questioned her. They never did.

Andreas stood nearby, the girls now sitting on the grass with their candy untouched in their laps. Cecilia's gaze passed over them, a small nod of approval exchanged between them. The architect and her model family.

The music swelled again. Cecilia clapped her hands twice, sharp and efficient, guiding the children into a ring around the maypole. She joined them for a step or two, then stepped back — watching, ensuring it all stayed in motion.

Patrik caught her eye for a moment. Her smile didn't falter, but there was no warmth in it. Just the satisfaction of a job well done. Of a village kept busy enough not to remember.

A gust of wind lifted the edge of her skirt. She smoothed it down without looking, already turning to adjust the speaker volume. The song played on — cheerful, familiar, and just loud enough to drown out anything that didn't belong to the day.

The song faded into polite applause. Tomas Nylander stood near the edge of the crowd, his hands clasped loosely in front of him. The collar of his shirt sat just visible beneath a casual jacket, a concession to the warmth of the day. His round glasses caught the sunlight as he nodded to a passing couple.

Someone handed him a paper cup. He didn't ask what was in it.

He nodded, said thanks, and didn't drink.

Cecilia passed him, her clipboard now tucked under one arm. She didn't stop, just gave him a glance and a satisfied nod. Tomas returned it, the same polite curve of the lips, nothing more. His eyes followed her for a moment before settling on the maypole where children stumbled through another round of dance.

Andreas stood nearby, exchanging words with a neighbor. Tomas' gaze touched on him, then moved away — too quickly to be noticed, too slow to be accidental. The cup in his hand remained untouched.

A boy ran past, nearly colliding with him. Tomas stepped aside, offering a muted chuckle that didn't reach his eyes. The boy's mother called an apology over her shoulder. Tomas raised a hand in response — a gesture that said everything was fine, even if it wasn't.

He sipped the drink at last. Lukewarm and too sweet. His smile held steady as another villager approached, launching into a story about last year's rain-soaked Midsummer. Tomas listened, nodding in the right places, his gaze drifting back to the girls in white dresses sitting too quietly by the grass.

The grill smoke drifted toward the far side of the green, where Patrik stood alone. A lukewarm hot dog rested in his hand, forgotten after the first bite. The mustard had started to dry at the edges of the bread.

From here, the music was softer — dulled by distance and conversation. Laughter rose in waves, breaking against the quiet that settled around him. No one noticed he wasn't part of it. That was the way Keldarp worked. If you stood still long enough, you became part of the scenery.

His eyes followed the slow orbit of villagers around the maypole. Bright dresses, swaying shirts, flower crowns tilting as the dance lost its rhythm and found it again. Children shouted verses out of sync, adults smiled as if they didn't hear the discord.

Andreas was easy to spot — taller than most, his daughters trailing behind him now, their hands clasped together. The white sleeves still covered their arms, even as other children shed layers under the afternoon sun.

Patrik shifted his weight, the gravel crunching under his shoe. He glanced down at the hot dog, then tossed it into a nearby bin without ceremony. The taste of it lingered — salt and something too sweet.

Cecilia's voice carried again, announcing the next game. Applause followed, automatic and eager. Tomas stood near the church path, still smiling, still nodding. The script held.

Patrik let his gaze drift across the scene one last time. The flower crowns, the leafy pole, the forced lightness that hung heavier than silence. He knew what they were really celebrating — not joy, but the relief of having something to hide behind.

A breeze caught the edge of the tablecloths, lifting them before they settled back into place. The village danced. Patrik stayed where he was.

The circle tightened around the maypole. Hands linked, feet moving in uneven steps across the worn grass. The speaker played "Små grodorna" now — the one about little frogs with no ears, no tails. Bright and foolish. Children bounced in time. Grown-ups smiled and sang along, as if they didn't hear themselves. The melody faltered for a second before returning. No one seemed to notice.

Children led the way, their voices high and breathless. Adults followed, slower, but smiling where they were expected to. Flower crowns slipped, petals scattered in the dirt. The scent of crushed grass mixed with sweat and barbecue smoke.

Andreas moved among them, Elsa and Maja at his sides. Their small hands gripped those of other villagers, drawn into the rhythm like everyone else. The girls' faces were blank — not unhappy, just elsewhere. Long sleeves brushing against bare arms without comment.

Cecilia stood near the speaker, clapping in time, her eyes scanning the circle to ensure no one strayed too far from the pattern. Tomas lingered at the edge, his smile steady, his gaze unfocused.

Patrik watched as the circle turned. The laughter grew louder, not from joy but from momentum — as if the sound itself could drown out memory. Feet stomped harder, voices rose with each verse, desperate to fill the space where truth might settle.

A gust of wind bent the tall grass beyond the green. The maypole stood firm, its decorations fluttering — bright distractions against a sky too clear to offer cover.

The dance went on. Around and around, as if movement alone could keep everything buried. No one looked beyond the circle. No one needed to. The music was loud enough.

Patrik stayed still, the only one not moving. The only one who knew that beneath every step, the ground wasn't holding the weight — it was swallowing it.

CHAPTER 22

Day of Silence

Patrik's steps slowed as the gravel thinned beneath his boots. The house stood ahead — a shape more than a home in the fading light. Blinds drawn. No movement. No sound but the distant bark of a dog, too far away to matter.

The air was heavy. Damp in a way that clung to the skin, pressing against him like a held breath. He stopped without meaning to, eyes fixed on the front door. Nothing unusual. No broken window. No sign of distress. Just a silence that felt too complete.

His hand hovered at his side. The instinct to walk up, to knock, was there — faint but persistent. Procedure whispered in the back of his mind, telling him there was nothing to justify it. No call. No report. Just stillness, and the weight of something not quite right.

A curtain might have moved. Or maybe it didn't. Hard to tell in this light. Patrik's gaze lingered, waiting for a reason to step forward. None came.

The gravel beneath his feet shifted as he adjusted his stance. The sound was too loud in the quiet. He glanced at the windows again — all closed, all covered. The kind of quiet that didn't belong to evening routines, but to something else. Something waiting.

He stayed there longer than he should have. Watching. Listening. Feeling the urge rise and settle again, like a wave that never quite broke.

Then, without a word, he let his hand fall back to his pocket. The silence held its ground.

Patrik's gaze lingered on the house a moment longer, then he turned. No sudden movement. Just a quiet decision, settled without ceremony.

The gravel gave way beneath his boots, soft and uneven. The house stayed behind him, unchanged. Blinds still drawn. Curtains still still. The kind of stillness that didn't confirm anything — but didn't ease anything either.

At the edge of the property, where the gravel met the cracked asphalt of the village road, he stopped. One breath. Then another. The air held a faint trace of woodsmoke — someone starting a fire early. It clung to the back of his throat, oddly sweet.

He adjusted the zipper of his jacket, not because of the cold, but for something to do. Fingers brushed fabric, then dropped. No hurry. No reason to rush.

His eyes didn't drift back. Whatever needed seeing, he'd already seen. Whatever hadn't shown itself — wouldn't. Not yet.

Then he walked on. Quiet steps, deliberate pace. Nothing urgent. Nothing wrong.

Just a house. Just a silence. Just another evening in Keldarp.

CHAPTER 23

Tobbe Knows

The late sun stretched shadows across the cracked asphalt. Plastic chairs outside Napoli sat half-occupied, their faded colors blending into the background hum of village life. Somewhere down the street, a lawnmower droned on — steady, indifferent.

Aram leaned against the counter inside, visible through the open door, handing over a pack of snus and scratch tickets without looking up. The customer muttered thanks, already scratching before he stepped outside.

The scent of fry oil hung in the air, mixing with cut grass and distant cigarette smoke. A sharp flick — someone lit up near the bus stop, where two teenagers laughed too loudly at something neither of them would remember tomorrow.

Patrik stood still, watching a woman in a floral dress load groceries into the back of a rusted Volvo. She closed the trunk with her hip, glanced around, and exchanged a nod with a passerby. No urgency. No whispers. Just another warm afternoon where nothing was wrong — because no one admitted that it was.

A child's bike lay abandoned on the pavement, its front wheel slowly spinning. From inside Napoli, the low murmur of a football commentary drifted out, ignored by everyone except the empty chairs facing the screen.

The village carried on — as it always did. Routine wrapped tight around everything, like plastic film over leftovers no one wanted to admit had gone bad. Patrik let the sounds settle — the buzz of conversation, the scrape of a chair, the hollow clink of a bottle against concrete.

No one looked his way. No one asked questions. The air was too full of everyday things to make space for anything else.

The flicker of movement caught Patrik's eye before the smell did — sharp tobacco curling through the air, cutting through the grease and grass. Tobbe was there, leaning against the brick wall of Napoli like he'd grown out of it, one boot crossed over the other, cigarette resting between two fingers.

No greeting. Just a glance — enough to register, not enough to invite conversation.

The village noise kept its rhythm. A screen door slammed somewhere. The hum of an engine coughed to life before settling into idle. A dog barked twice, then thought better of it.

Patrik didn't move. Neither did Tobbe. The space between them filled with smoke and the weight of things neither wanted to say first.

Tobbe's hand moved — a slow drag, exhale through his nose. The smoke drifted sideways, catching the late sun, before disappearing into nothing. His eyes stayed fixed on the street, watching nothing in particular. Just watching.

Patrik shifted his weight, hands in his pockets, feeling the rough edge of his keys against his thumb. The sharp flick of Tobbe's lighter sounded again — unnecessary, but habitual. The cigarette burned steady.

Another family passed by, plastic bags swinging, nodding politely without stopping. Normal. Everything normal.

Tobbe didn't look at Patrik. He didn't need to. The waiting wasn't for Patrik to arrive — it was for the moment when silence had done enough work.

The cigarette burned low, ash clinging stubbornly to the tip. Tobbe let it hang between his fingers, the smoke curling upward in thin threads. The village sounds blurred into background hum — a lawnmower sputtered to a stop, replaced by the distant chatter of two men discussing football odds.

Tobbe's voice broke through, flat and low.

"It's too damn quiet."

The words hung there, heavier than the smoke. No glance toward Patrik. No need. It wasn't a comment — it was a verdict.

Patrik's eyes followed a sparrow hopping along the edge of the pavement, pecking at nothing. A car rolled past, slow enough to nod at, but the driver didn't bother.

Tobbe brought the cigarette back to his lips, inhaled like it was routine — like he hadn't just said what no one else dared to. When he spoke again, it was almost casual.

"He killed her."

The smoke drifted sideways, catching in the late light before dissolving. No emphasis. No drama. Just fact, spoken aloud because pretending otherwise had run its course.

Patrik didn't answer. The village didn't pause. Somewhere behind them, Aram's voice called out an order number. A bottle clinked against another in a recycling bin.

The truth didn't need repeating. It was already there — in the quiet, in the way no one asked questions, in the way summer warmth couldn't quite cover the rot beneath.

The last of Tobbe's cigarette crumbled under his boot, ground into the gravel with a slow twist. The smoke lingered longer than it should have, drifting between them before fading into the warm air.

Patrik's gaze stayed on the horizon — where Road 46 cut through the village like it always had, indifferent to what lay on either side. A cyclist passed, head down, a plastic bag dangling from the handlebar. The world kept moving.

Tobbe didn't say more. He didn't have to. The weight of his words pressed down, not expecting argument — just waiting to see if Patrik would carry it too.

Patrik shifted his stance, feeling the stiffness in his shoulders. His jaw tightened — a brief flicker of resistance, habit more than doubt. Then it passed.

He nodded. Once. Barely more than a tilt of the head, but enough.

Tobbe caught it in the corner of his eye and gave the faintest grunt — approval, or maybe just acknowledgment that the lie they'd both lived with was done now.

A breeze stirred the faded parasols outside Napoli. Somewhere, a door creaked open and shut again. Life continued around them, unchanged.

But between the two of them, the silence had shifted. The time for pretending was over.

The nod settled between them like a final breath. Nothing more to say. Nothing left to wait for.

Patrik straightened. His eyes fixed on the road ahead — not the street, not the village, but the stretch that led past the allotments, past the edge of the familiar. Toward the house with drawn curtains.

He didn't look at Tobbe. Just stepped forward. One foot, then the other. Controlled. Measured. No urgency, but no pause.

The village sounds faded behind him — the hum of small engines, laughter from Napoli, the muted clatter of cutlery indoors. All of it stayed where it was.

Tobbe didn't follow.

Patrik kept walking. Past the faded bus stop, past the mailbox half-swallowed by weeds. Gravel crunched beneath his boots in the same steady rhythm he'd learned long ago — on patrol, in pursuit, at scenes that waited just long enough to be noticed too late.

The wind shifted. Cooler now. Quiet in a different way.

He wasn't carrying his Police ID. No weapon. Nothing to mark him as police. Just a man, walking toward something that couldn't be ignored any longer. Not angry. Not panicking. Determined.

Up ahead, Andreas Karlsson's house waited — silent, unremarkable, as if nothing had ever happened there.

Patrik didn't slow.

CHAPTER 24

The House

The road had no name. Just a strip of gravel curving past forgotten fences and untrimmed hedges. Patrik walked it without sound, the soles of his boots muting against packed dirt and scattered leaves. The evening air was thick — not humid, not warm — just full. Like it held something back.

The house didn't look different. That was part of it. Curtains still drawn. Paint still peeling along the frame where no one cared enough to sand. A garden hose coiled like a dead snake in the grass. One of the stepping stones tilted slightly — a detail no one else would notice, but he did.

The car was parked further up the road, just out of sight. Intentional. This wasn't official. Not anymore.

He reached the gate, unlatched it quietly. The hinges didn't squeal — someone had oiled them once. A long time ago. It swung in without resistance. Gravel shifted under his weight, crunching with a rhythm that felt too slow, like something dragging its heels.

The porch sagged in the middle. He stepped around the spot where the wood had started to rot, even though no one had told him it had. The doormat said "Welcome," faded and curling at the edges.

He stood there a moment. Just stood. The silence wasn't peaceful. It pushed back. Inside the house — behind the door — the stillness waited. Heavy. Decaying. Dense with something unsaid.

He looked at his hand. Not shaking. Just there. Then he stepped forward, toward the door, like there was no other option. Like he'd known for days this was where he'd end up.

The air had thickened. Clouds hung lower now, pressing down like an unanswered question. Patrik stood before the door — close enough to see where the wood had warped around the old brass handle, where someone's knuckles had once worn a patch smooth.

He raised his hand. Not quick, not slow. Just steady. Fingers curled, until it was just his fist. He knocked once. Nothing loud. Nothing that demanded. Just contact — dull and dry, the sound absorbed by the door like water into rotten cloth.

Then silence. Not the absence of noise, but the refusal of response. Inside, the house held its breath. No footsteps. No voices. Not even the creak of a floorboard.

He waited. Hand falling back to his side. Not checking the windows. Not calling out. Just still. Like waiting had to be done, even if it wouldn't change anything.

The knock wasn't hope. It was formality. A gesture made because it was expected. Because once, in a better version of the world, someone might have answered.

Now, it was just the echo of a role he no longer played — the man with questions, the man who might save something. He knew better. That part was finished.

He looked once at the handle. Then down. Then forward again. No sigh. No words. Just standing there, in a moment that had already passed.

Clouds pressed lower now. The light had shifted — less gray, more yellow at the edges, like bruised fruit. Patrik's hand moved without instruction. Not sudden. Not reluctant. Just forward, until his palm rested flat against the door.

It felt dry. Warped slightly under pressure. The grain caught at his skin, ridges like old scars. For a moment, he didn't move. Just held it. Not to feel — there was nothing to feel — but to register that the moment had arrived. The space between knowing and doing had vanished.

No second breath. No glance behind. Just the weight of his body shifting forward, enough to press. Enough to test.

The door gave a little. Not much. A fraction. As if it remembered what it was supposed to do but had grown tired of doing it.

His fingers shifted position. Palm to grip. Thumb along the edge. The movement was slow, practiced. Not like someone forcing entry. More like someone coming home, without the key, knowing it didn't matter anymore.

He leaned into it — not with strength, but with finality. The wood creaked low. Not loud. Not resisting. Just speaking, softly, like houses do when they've been waiting too long for someone to come back.

The door yielded without ceremony. A slow grind as wood scraped past swollen frame, the hinges groaning low like a warning meant for someone else. The edge caught briefly — then gave. A final sigh before opening wide enough to pass.

Patrik stepped forward. Not cautiously. Not bold either. Just the same pace he'd used walking up. The same weight in his shoes. He crossed the threshold like he had every right, even if none of it belonged to him. Not anymore.

The air didn't move. Inside, it pressed inward — stale and thick, like something waiting just out of sight. No light welcomed him. The hallway swallowed what little the sky offered, fading into a dense gray that had stopped being shadow and become substance.

Paint peeled in long strips down the far wall. A boot print marked the floor — dry, dusty, not his. Probably old. Probably.

He didn't reach for the light switch. Didn't need it. The darkness didn't hide anything he didn't already know. He paused just inside. Let the door fall shut behind him. The sound echoed down the hall — soft, final, untouched by wind.

One step, then another. No urgency. Just movement. Just a man in a house where something had already happened, long before he got there.

It hit him halfway down the hall. No warning. Just there — sudden and thick, like something crawling up from the floorboards. The smell of rot, damp and cloying, layered with sour milk and something sharper. Human. Undeniable.

He stopped. Not out of shock. Not surprise. Just to let the wave pass. His mouth stayed shut. Breathing through the nose didn't help. The air offered no escape. It pressed against the back of his throat, filled the soft tissue behind the eyes. A presence, not a scent.

Somewhere behind a closed door, a fly buzzed — steady, circling, insistent. Another joined. Then silence. Then back again. The rhythm of a room that hadn't been entered. Not in time.

Patrik didn't flinch. Didn't cover his face. His hands stayed at his sides. He looked ahead. Toward the door at the end of the hall. Closed, but not locked. A thin shadow beneath it told him what he already knew.

He let the moment settle. Let the house breathe around him. The walls didn't creak. Nothing shifted. Even the flies seemed to wait, suspended mid-air like they were listening too.

The smell didn't change. It didn't need to. He had smelled it before. Different rooms. Different lives. Same truth.

The door opened with the quiet of something long unbothered. No resistance. Just a shift in weight, a murmur of hinges. Patrik stepped through.

Outside, a car passed on Road 46 — a soft whir, a quick blur of tires. Then silence again. The kind Keldarp kept around itself like a blanket. Heavy. Familiar.

Patrik closed the door behind him. No slam. Just the click of wood on wood. He didn't lock it.

CHAPTER 25

The Scene

The smell came first. Not blood — that would come later — but the sour musk of sweat and beer and something else. A rot that had started long before the body stopped breathing.

Andreas lay on the floor between the kitchen and hallway. One arm curled under him, the other outstretched toward the threshold. Face down. Head open. Skull cracked wide where the buckshot had exited, tearing through bone and wall. A spray of grey and red had settled on the linoleum. Some had dried. Some hadn't.

His shirt had ridden up. Pale skin pressed against the vinyl tiles. A thin trail of urine had leaked from beneath him, soaking into the seam of a rug. No signs of struggle. Just gravity and finality.

The refrigerator hummed behind him. A bottle rolled gently in place each time the compressor kicked on. The fly buzzing near his ear had landed now. Others joined it. They crawled along his hairline and into the wound with the patience of things that don't need to rush.

The shotgun lay against the wall. Not dropped — placed. Leaned carefully, barrel pointing down, safety still off. The stock dark with something sticky.

No note. No explanation. Just what was left. What couldn't be denied anymore.

They were pressed against him. One on each side. Small limbs folded into the curve of his body like they might keep him warm. Or keep themselves from slipping away.

Elsa had her face buried against him. The flannel of his shirt was soaked through — not just with blood, but with urine, with sweat, with the stink of something long gone. Her fingers were tangled in the fabric, knuckles white, as if to loosen them would mean letting go of something final. Maja was half beneath his outstretched arm, her cheek resting on the floor, eyes open. Not blinking. Holding a stuffed rabbit. Covered in blood. Stained by feces.

Neither moved. Not when the door creaked. Not when a boot scraped the entryway. Not even when the flies began to gather again, drawn to the stillness like they knew it now belonged to them.

The girls were barefoot. Dirt smeared up their calves, black crescents beneath their nails. Elsa's diaper and pants were completely soaked through, the cotton clinging to her legs like wet paper. Maja had nothing on her lower half. Just a long t-shirt, too thin for the season. She was smeared all over with her own feces and urine.

No sound came from them. Not even breath you could hear. Just the slow collapse of what should never have been asked of children. If they had noticed Patrik, they didn't acknowledge it.

At some point, Elsa let go of Andreas.

Not all at once. Her fingers loosened in stages, hesitant and slow. Like pulling free from something sticky. She shifted her weight onto her knees, leaving a damp, datk patch behind on the floor. The silence stayed with her. Clung tighter than the shirt.

The shotgun was laying where it had fallen — on the floor between his legs. Elsa's hand moved toward it without looking at anything else. No glance to her sister. No pause at the blood.

She placed her hand on the cold steel. As if to show it Patrik. As if it was the only way she could acknowledge that they were not alone anymore. The hand reached around the barrel. Not a grab — a touch. Just fingers against cold metal. She held it there. Not long. Not short. Just enough. Then let go.

There was no expression on her face. No curiosity, no fear. The kind of look worn by people who've already seen the worst of it. Her fingers left a faint smudge on the barrel. A trace of feces, of urine, of something human.

Behind her, Maja hadn't moved. The stuffed rabbit now lay on its side in a puddle of something that was probably water. Or milk. Or not.

Patik didn't move. He just observed. For a full minute, before reaching for his phone and calling dispatch.

Then he just stood there again. Not comforting the girls. Not trying to calm them. Not investigating the scene. He just waited.

The lights came first — blue pulses thrown across the windows, crawling across the wallpaper like something alive. Then the crunch of gravel, the slam of doors, the low murmur of radio traffic barely muffled by glass.

Patrik stepped back, clearing the hallway with a nod. No words. No gestures. Just space made for what came next.

Two paramedics entered first. Boots squeaking on the linoleum, latex gloves already on. One carried a red trauma bag he wouldn't open. The other looked at Andreas for less than a second before turning away. Their job wasn't for the dead.

Behind them, a uniformed officer — young, unfamiliar. Clipboard in hand, eyes wide but mouth shut. He moved like someone walking into cold water. Slowly, carefully, pretending not to feel the cold.

The girls hadn't moved. Not when the door opened. Not now. Maja's head lolled against Elsa's shoulder, mouth slightly open. Elsa stared straight ahead. Past the living. Past the dead.

One of the medics crouched down, hand on his knee. "Vitals," he said. Not to anyone in particular. The other one was already writing.

The system had arrived. Not to fix. Just to clean up.

Outside, an unmarked Volvo idled. The exhaust curled in the cooling air, vanishing before it reached the ditch.

Inside the house, the girls were wrapped in grey fleece blankets. Standard issue — clean, neutral, anonymous. Maja was carried. Elsa walked, but only because they asked her to. She didn't look at anyone. Just moved forward like she was being led through a tunnel no one else could see.

The woman from Social Services didn't introduce herself. She didn't crouch down to speak. She signed the form, nodded once, and took the younger one first. A medic helped with the door.

Patrik watched from the hallway. He didn't follow them out. No one asked him to. He noted the time. That was the procedure.

Elsa paused at the door. Only for a second. Not enough to say anything. Not enough to make it matter. Then she stepped outside and was gone.

The woman buckled them in. One car seat. One booster. The doors closed with the soft mechanical click of a leased vehicle. No urgency. No comfort.

"We'll process them in Ulricehamn," someone said. Not to Patrik. Just aloud.

The car pulled away without sirens. Just taillights shrinking into dark.

CHAPTER 26

The Report

The cursor blinked in the corner of the screen. A small, insistent reminder that the words weren't going to type themselves.

Patrik adjusted his glasses, though they didn't need adjusting. The frames had started to leave a mark on the bridge of his nose. He let his fingers find their place on the keyboard. Familiar keys. Familiar task.

Andreas Karlsson. Born 14 March 1986.

The soft clatter of plastic on plastic filled the room, swallowed by the hum of the overhead lights. Patrik paused. His reflection stared back faintly from the dark edge of the monitor — pale skin, tired eyes, beard overdue for a trim.

Sofia Karlsson-Lindqvist. Born 22 November 1990. Missing, presumed dead.

The words looked clean on the screen. Neutral. Stripped of everything that mattered. He reached for the coffee mug beside him. Lukewarm. Stale. He drank anyway.

Elsa Karlsson, age 3. Maja Karlsson, age 2. Found alive.

His fingers hesitated at the period. A full stop. As if that ended something.

Patrik leaned back slightly, eyes scanning the lines he had flattened into procedure. Blood, fear, the smell of rot — all gone. Replaced by dates, names, and passive verbs. No need to mention how long the girls had sat there. No need to describe the way Elsa had held the shotgun like it was a toy.

The fluorescent light above flickered. Once. Twice. Then steadied again.

He returned to the keyboard. There was more to file. Always more.

The cursor blinked once more before Patrik's hand drifted toward the mouse. He saved the draft without thinking. Muscle memory.

The phone vibrated before it rang — a low hum against the cluttered desk. Papers shifted slightly. A pen rolled, stopped against his wrist.

He let it ring twice. Watched the screen light up with a number he didn't recognize. Local from Ulricehamn.

On the third ring, he picked up. The receiver felt heavier at this hour.

"Bockgren." His voice was steady. Stripped of anything personal.

The voice on the other end was polite. Practiced. Words chosen for efficiency, not comfort. Patrik listened, eyes fixed on a coffee stain bleeding into a stack of forms. District court. Temporarily appointed guardian for the children.

He spoke of procedures. Declarations. Timelines. Sofia's name used like a reference number — something to be processed, not mourned.

Patrik didn't interrupt. His thumb traced the edge of a sticky note, folding the corner over and back again.

A pause on the line. The kind where the other person expects acknowledgment.

"I understand," he said. It was all they needed.

The voice continued, softer now — as if discussing something delicate. But it was the same script. Just quieter.

The phone's glow faded as the call stretched on. The only light left came from the monitor, where unfinished sentences waited.

The voice on the line shifted to business. The softness was gone. Patrik reached for a pen without looking, found it by instinct, and dragged a notepad closer.

"Normally it takes five years to declare a missing person dead. But with strong suspicion that Andreas killed her, we can proceed in a year."

The pen moved. The words came out uniform, detached. His handwriting didn't falter — it never did when it mattered least.

The official listed requirements. Statements to be phrased carefully. Patrik underlined a date without thinking. A line too neat for what it represented.

Outside the thin window, the dark pressed in. No sense of time — just the hollow quiet of a building long past office hours.

"If the report emphasizes the likelihood," the voice continued, "it'll smooth the process. The girls can be declared orphans. The practicalities can be dealt with."

Patrik wrote that down too, though he didn't need to. His eyes followed the ink, not the meaning.

A pause. Paper shuffling on the other end. The sound of someone clearing their throat, preparing to move on to the next case once this call ended.

"Do you foresee any complications?"

Patrik's gaze settled on the computer screen. The names waiting there. The half-finished sentence blinking at him.

"No," he said. His voice as flat as the paper in front of him.

The conversation drifted to confirmations. Email addresses. Deadlines. Patrik noted them all, his pen steady, his mind elsewhere.

The guardian wrapped up with the practiced tone of someone offering closure.

"It'll be better for the girls. Help them move on."

Patrik didn't answer right away. His eyes followed the curve of his own handwriting — neat lines that meant nothing once filed away.

The receiver felt lighter as he lowered it. The soft click of plastic meeting wood was the only acknowledgment.

Silence settled back into the room. Not peace — just absence.

He let his hand rest on the phone for a moment longer, fingers brushing over the buttons as if there might be more to say. There wasn't.

The notes lay in front of him, precise and useless. He stacked them without care, aligning the edges out of habit rather than purpose.

The screen's glow pulled his attention back. The report still open, cursor waiting. The same names staring back at him.

Patrik reached for the coffee cup again. Cold now. He drank anyway.

The hum of the fluorescent lights above filled the space where the voice had been. Routine reclaimed everything.

He placed the phone back in its cradle — soft, deliberate. Another task completed. Another truth folded into procedure.

The phone sat quiet. The papers were stacked. The coffee gone cold twice over.

Patrik's eyes fixed on the screen. The cursor blinked at the end of the report — patient, indifferent.

He read the last sentence again. Each word chosen for clarity. For neutrality. Nothing misplaced. Nothing true.

His hand hovered over the keyboard, but there was nothing left to add. The facts were typed. The story sealed.

The glow from the monitor cast a pale light across his hands — steady, practiced hands. The same hands that had lifted Elsa from the floor. That had pulled the shotgun from her grasp.

Now they rested on the desk. Still. Useless.

Outside the window, darkness pressed against the glass. The world beyond didn't care what was written here.

Patrik let the silence stretch. The hum of electricity. The faint tick of the wall clock he didn't bother to check.

The cursor blinked. Waiting for him to finish what was already done.

He didn't move. Just sat there — watching as the truth disappeared into the shape of a report no one would question.

CHAPTER 27

The Eulogy

The church smelled of lilies and old wood. A faint chill hung in the air, untouched by the handful of candles flickering near the altar. Patrik sat two rows from the front, hands resting on his knees, eyes fixed on the single coffin. Light filtered through stained glass in muted colors, too dim to offer warmth.

Beside the coffin, there was nothing. Just empty space where another should have been. The absence pressed heavier than the polished wood.

The villagers filled the pews with quiet efficiency — dark coats, bowed heads, the rustle of order. No tears. No whispers. Only the sound of shoes scuffing against stone as they settled into place. It wasn't mourning. It was maintenance. A community tidying up the story before it frayed at the edges.

Tomas stood near the pulpit, eyes lowered, fingers adjusting his collar as if buying time. Cecilia sat in her usual place — front row, centered — her back straight, hands folded neatly in her lap. Her expression was calm. Practiced. The kind worn by someone who understood that grief, like everything else, should be kept within proper boundaries.

Patrik shifted his gaze back to the coffin. The varnish caught what little light there was, reflecting nothing of the man inside. A lid closed too soon for one, too late for the other. Closure, they'd call it. Even if half of what needed burying had never been found.

The church door creaked once more before falling shut. The last of them had arrived. Silence settled — not heavy, but expected. Routine. Patrik exhaled through his nose and waited, like everyone else, for the truth to be packed away properly.

The silence held a moment longer, stretched thin beneath the vaulted ceiling. Then Tomas moved. Slow steps to the pulpit, each one echoing against stone and wood. He rested his hands on either side of the lectern, fingers splayed, knuckles pale.

Patrik watched the priest's gaze sweep across the congregation — not searching for comfort, but measuring how much truth they would tolerate.

"We gather today," Tomas began, his voice steady but stripped of ceremony, "not because we have all the answers."

The words drifted through the dim air, brushing against the villagers like an unwelcome draft. No one shifted. No one met his eyes.

"We say farewell to Andreas Karlsson," Tomas continued, his tone careful, as if each word weighed more than it should. "And we acknowledge... the absence of Sofia Karlsson-Lindqvist."

A pause. Longer than polite. Patrik saw Cecilia's jaw tighten, her hands folding a fraction tighter in her lap. Someone in the back cleared their throat, too loud in the quiet.

"There are things we will never know," Tomas said, voice carrying just enough to fill the space without pressing. "But we do know this — darkness doesn't arrive uninvited. It grows where we let it."

The stained glass above him cast dull patterns across his shoulders, like bruises in colored light. Tomas didn't flinch. He stood there, holding the village's gaze without demanding it.

"Today, we do not pretend. We lay to rest what can be laid to rest."

Another pause. The weight of what he didn't say pressed harder than the words themselves. Patrik felt it settle in his chest — the simple, careful honesty that wouldn't last past the church doors.

Tomas bowed his head. No flourish. No comfort offered. Just the echo of truth, left hanging in the cold air.

The final echoes of Tomas' words faded into the rafters, leaving only the sound of breathing and the faint creak of old pews under shifting weight. No one spoke. No one moved to wipe a tear that hadn't come.

Patrik let his eyes drift over the rows ahead. Shoulders stiff beneath worn jackets. Hands folded too neatly, gripping order like a lifeline. A man near the aisle glanced at his watch, the motion small but telling. Another fiddled with the corner of a hymn book, thumb running along the frayed edge as if searching for a page that wouldn't be read today.

Cecilia remained still, her posture unbroken. But even she let her gaze drop — not in reflection, but in quiet calculation of when this would be over.

A cough from somewhere near the back. The scrape of a shoe repositioned. Eyes fixed on the coffin or on nothing at all. Tomas had spoken plainly, but the village wore his honesty like an ill-fitting suit — tolerated because it was required, not because it belonged here.

Patrik felt the weight of it — the collective endurance. They could sit through truth, as long as it kept to its place and didn't linger too long. An hour, maybe less, and it would be folded away with the hymn sheets and the scent of lilies.

Outside, the grey light pressed against the stained glass, dull and persistent. No salvation in it. Just another reminder that the service would end soon, and with it, the brief allowance for discomfort.

Someone shifted again. A whispered word passed between two women in the second row — not about what was said, but likely about the coffee waiting next door. The important things.

Patrik straightened his back and let the silence stretch. This was as much honesty as Keldarp would permit. And even that was already fading.

The clink of porcelain replaced the silence of the church. In the parish hall, voices returned — low at first, then growing into the familiar murmur of routine. Patrik stood near the doorway, the scent of overbrewed coffee and almond cake settling around him like a worn blanket.

Tables lined with pastries and biscuits offered comfort where words had failed. A silver tray of cinnamon buns sat half-empty already, the sugar glistening under weak fluorescent lights.

Someone laughed — not loud, but enough to remind everyone that life was expected to continue.

Patrik watched as plates were filled, cups passed along with nods and polite smiles. Tomas stood by the window, alone, his hands wrapped around a cup he hadn't touched. His gaze fixed somewhere beyond the glass, where the overcast sky pressed down on gravestones and trimmed hedges.

Cecilia moved through the room with practiced ease, a soft word here, a guiding hand there. Her smile never faltered — calm, composed, as if the eulogy had been nothing more than a necessary formality. She refilled cups, straightened napkins, and steered conversations back to safer ground.

Snippets of talk floated past Patrik. Weather. The summer party. The price of diesel. Sofia's name didn't surface. Neither did Andreas'. The coffin was already fading — replaced by sponge cake and the comfort of things that didn't demand reflection.

Patrik accepted a cup from a woman he barely recognized. He nodded his thanks, though neither of them spoke. The bitterness of the coffee grounded him. Across the room, a group chuckled softly over some forgotten anecdote, their backs already turned on the morning's honesty.

The hum of conversation thickened. Chairs scraped against linoleum. Spoons stirred without purpose. The village had found its rhythm again — the ritual working as it always did. Patrik sipped his coffee and let the noise wash over him. Reflection was no longer required.

The plate in Patrik's hand was empty now, the remnants of a cinnamon bun reduced to a few stray crumbs. The coffee had gone cold. Around him, the parish hall buzzed with quiet chatter, chairs pushed back as people began to drift toward the door.

Cecilia found him before he could move. She appeared at his side, smooth as always, her smile already in place — the kind that didn't invite response, only acceptance.

"Tomas had to say what he did," she said, her voice low enough to seem personal, but loud enough to carry if needed. Her eyes scanned the room, not meeting his. "But now it's time to move forward."

Patrik looked at her, saying nothing. The words weren't meant for discussion. They were a verdict — calm, absolute.

Cecilia's hands rested lightly on the edge of the table, fingers aligning a stack of napkins that didn't need straightening. Her posture was relaxed, practiced in the art of appearing at ease while ensuring everything stayed in its proper place.

She glanced at him then — brief, measured — before her gaze moved on, already assessing who else might need reminding of the correct way to carry grief.

"It's what's best," she added, almost as an afterthought, before stepping away with the same composed grace, her presence leaving a faint trace of lavender and authority behind.

Patrik remained where he was, the cold cup still in his hand. Around him, conversations resumed — talk of weekend plans, borrowed tools, the ordinary weight of village life returning to its axis.

Cecilia's footsteps faded into the murmur of the parish hall. Patrik set his cup down, untouched since her words. The tablecloth beneath it was patterned with small stains — old coffee rings, traces of gatherings past. Nothing ever washed out completely here.

The chairs were filling again. Not with mourners, but with neighbors reclaiming routine. Someone asked about the hay harvest. Another mentioned a cousin's upcoming wedding in Falköping. Laughter — soft, but genuine — rose from a corner where two men discussed engine trouble.

Patrik stood still, watching as the room stitched itself back together. Tomas had disappeared, the black of his cassock no longer visible among the muted sweaters and worn jackets. Cecilia's calm voice floated above the rest now and then, smoothing over any lingering edges.

Outside the window, the sky pressed down in its uniform grey. A sparrow landed on the sill, pecked at nothing, then flew off — unnoticed by anyone but Patrik.

The coffin was already far from their minds. Sofia's absence even further. The village had done what it came to do. The story was boxed, sealed, and stored where it wouldn't interfere with afternoon chores or evening television.

Patrik let his gaze drift across the room one last time. Conversations carried on, plates refilled, the weight of the morning evaporating like breath in cold air.

He reached for his coat, the fabric heavy in his hands. No one looked his way as he moved toward the door. There was nothing left to say. The truth — like the man in the coffin — had been buried properly.

CHAPTER 28

Majvor's Candle

The match scraped against the box with a dry whisper. A brief flare — then the steady pulse of flame. Majvor shielded it with her hand, though there was no draft. The candle waited, wick already darkened from nights before. Routine made deliberate.

Majvor had normally switched to LED candles. Too many forgotten flames over the years. Too many close calls. But today she felt that only the real thing would do.

The flame caught with a soft sigh, curling upwards before settling into a quiet glow. She let the match burn low before pinching it out between her fingers. The faint scent of sulphur mixed with warm wax — familiar, unremarkable.

Outside the window, nothing moved. Darkness pressed against the glass, dense and patient. The village had long since surrendered to sleep. Doors locked, curtains drawn. Silence chosen.

Majvor adjusted the candle slightly, centering it on the windowsill. Not for aesthetics — just so the light would be seen, if anyone bothered to look. No prayer. No gesture. Only the flame, steady and small, where none was expected.

Her reflection hovered behind the glass — pale, lined, barely more than a shadow beside the flicker. She didn't meet her own eyes. Instead, she watched the flame until it stopped dancing, until it became part of the night's stillness.

Majvor pulled the chair closer to the window, the legs sliding softly against worn linoleum. The cushion sank beneath her as she sat, hands resting in her lap, empty and still.

The candle's glow stretched just far enough to touch the edges of the kitchen table. Beyond that — shadows. The cold coffee cup sat untouched, a ring of condensation marking where it had been earlier. The smell of wax thickened as the flame settled into its rhythm.

She watched the light, not the darkness beyond. The reflection in the glass blurred — flame and face merging, neither sharp enough to matter.

The house held its breath. No clock ticking, no pipes groaning. Only the faint crackle of the wick as it consumed itself slowly, without complaint.

Majvor's gaze didn't wander. The iPad on the counter stayed dark. The baking tins stacked neatly by the sink waited for morning. This moment wasn't for distraction or routine. It was for staying awake when others preferred to forget.

The flame flickered once, then steadied. Majvor's posture remained unchanged. She wasn't keeping vigil. She was simply refusing to look away.

The flame held steady, its reflection doubling in the glass. Beyond it, the village offered nothing back. No light. No movement. Just the weight of darkness pressing against the windowpane.

Majvor's eyes shifted, not to the flame this time, but past it — into the black where familiar shapes dissolved. She could trace where the church spire would be, where the empty road curved toward silence. But tonight, Keldarp had no edges. It had vanished into itself.

Somewhere out there, behind closed curtains and drawn blinds, people slept easy. Their dreams undisturbed by the things they'd chosen not to see. The kind of peace that came from looking away long enough that it felt natural.

The candle's light didn't reach them. It wasn't meant to.

Majvor didn't move. The cold had crept into her feet, but she let it. The flame would burn down in its own time. She wouldn't snuff it out.

Outside, the village held its breath — content, forgetful. Inside, the flame remained. Small. Unnoticed. But alive.

Someone had to remember.

CHAPTER 29

Tobbe and Patrik

The neon sign outside Napoli buzzed faintly, casting a dull red glow across the empty patio chairs. Inside, the fridge hummed. Out here on the terrace, a lone fly traced lazy circles above the plastic table where two bottles stood, sweating in the warmth of one of those rare summer nights that hadn't yet decided to cool down.

Patrik rested his forearms on the worn surface, fingers lightly touching the neck of his beer. Tobbe sat beside him, shoulders hunched forward, cap pulled low. No words passed between them. None were needed. The clink of glass as Aram cleared off an empty plastic table marked his quiet presence — efficient, unobtrusive. He knew better than to interrupt whatever this was.

The ashtray between them held the remains of Tobbe's cigarette. He hadn't lit another. Patrik's gaze followed the slow drift of smoke, then settled on the sticky, faded, laminated menu on the table. Same specials as always. Same prices scratched out and rewritten over the years.

The door creaked as a breeze pushed against it, but no one went in or out. Keldarp was already asleep, save for the low murmur of a distant tractor and the occasional chirp of something unseen.

Tobbe shifted, the plastic chair groaning under the movement. Patrik took a sip, the beer lukewarm now but easier that way. They hadn't planned this. They never did. Yet here they were — two men shaped by the same streets, the same silences, settling back into a rhythm that no longer needed explanation.

In the window, the neon open sign flickered once before steadying again.

A car passed on Road 46. The sound of tires against asphalt filling the gaps where conversation might have lived. Patrik traced a thumb over the label of his bottle, the print worn smooth from habit more than thought.

Tobbe's hand moved — not to his drink, but to his pocket. He fished out a crumpled pack, shook out a cigarette, then seemed to think better of it. The cigarette stayed between his fingers, unlit. His gaze fixed somewhere beyond the counter, where the neon glow met the dark window and reflected two men who looked older than they remembered being.

"Fuck Andreas." The words slipped out, flat and quiet, like stating the weather.

Patrik didn't look over. The words weren't meant for a response.

Tobbe rolled the cigarette between his fingers, eyes still locked on nothing. "Kids shouldn't have to go through that."

The sentence hung there, heavier than the stale beer smell and the smoke that never came. Aram glanced up from wiping a tray but didn't linger. He knew the kind of talk best left alone.

Tobbe finally set the cigarette down beside the ashtray. His fingers tapped the glass bottle once, then twice — a dull rhythm that didn't need finishing.

Another car drove by. The night pressed on darker now. Patient and indifferent. As dark as it gets this time of year. A dull purple glow on the horizon.

Tobbe's words faded, but they didn't leave. They settled into the cracks — between the clink of glass, the crickets, the faint buzz of the neon bleeding through the window.

Patrik let his eyes shift, slow and deliberate, to the man beside him. The same broad shoulders that once leaned over mopeds and stolen beers behind the gym hall. Same calloused hands, now resting on the counter, stained with oil and years that didn't need mentioning.

Tobbe didn't meet his gaze. He didn't need to. The line had been spoken — simple, clear, the kind of truth no one else in Keldarp dared to give voice to.

Patrik nodded once. Barely more than a tilt of the chin, but enough.

The patio parasols shifted in the breeze, their fabric faded from too many summers. Inside, nothing moved except for Dilan wiping down another table.

Patrik saw Tobbe now — not as the kid who once dared him to shoplift a pack of chewing gum, not as the man half the village dismissed as a relic with a temper. But as the only one who had spoken when it mattered. No speeches. No posturing. Just a quiet refusal to look away.

The silence between them wasn't empty. It held something earned.

Their bottles sat half-empty, the chill long gone. Tobbe reached for his first, lifting it without ceremony. A slow pull, then the soft thud of glass meeting wood again.

Patrik followed, the motion unthinking — the kind of rhythm built over years, where conversation was optional and silence did the heavy lifting.

Aram had disappeared into the back, leaving the terrace to them and the faint sound of crickets keeping the place alive past its prime hours. The smell of lilacs, mixing with the faint trace of cigarette smoke that never fully left Napoli's walls.

A moth battered itself against the neon light, frantic in a way that felt out of place here. Tobbe's fingers drummed once more against the glass before tipping it for the last mouthful.

Patrik let his own bottle drain, the taste flat but familiar. He set it down gently, the small sound louder than expected in the quiet.

No words marked the end of the drinks. No gesture to signal more. It wasn't that kind of night.

For a moment longer, they sat — two empty bottles between them, the weight of what had been said already enough.

Tobbe slid his stool back, the scrape of wood on tile breaking the stillness. He stood without a word, reaching for his wallet out of habit.

Aram reappeared, waving it off with a nod — a quiet understanding that this round wasn't counted in kronor.

Patrik rose a moment later. The air between them held no ceremony, just the weight of something settled. Tobbe extended his hand — rough, calloused, the grip of a man who worked with engines and metal more than people.

Patrik took it. Firm. Brief. No squeeze to prove anything, no lingering to add meaning. The kind of handshake that didn't need explanation.

Outside, the neon sign flickered again, casting broken light across the empty street. The hum of the fridge faded as its cycle ended, leaving a pocket of quiet that neither tried to fill.

Tobbe gave a small nod — not quite a farewell, more an acknowledgment. Patrik answered in kind.

The handshake said what neither of them would. Not gratitude. Not apology. Just a new found respect — the kind that didn't need to be spoken aloud in a place like Keldarp.

Then, without a glance back, Tobbe stepped off the terrace.

The night had settled deep — warm, still, the kind of quiet that pressed close but didn't suffocate.

For a moment, they stood side by side on the cracked pavement, the faint buzz of the neon sign and the distant hum of a streetlamp drawing moths into their endless orbit.

Tobbe adjusted his jacket, eyes fixed on the road ahead. Patrik glanced toward the QStar across the way, its pumps standing idle under a crooked sign.

No words passed between them. None were expected. The handshake had already said enough, and anything more would only cheapen it.

Tobbe stepped off first, boots striking the asphalt with steady purpose. He didn't look back.

Patrik watched him go until the shape of him blurred into the shadows between streetlights. Then he turned the other way, his own footsteps measured, unhurried.

The village around them slept, unaware or unwilling to notice the quiet line drawn tonight. No fanfare. No declarations. Just two figures parting ways under a sky that didn't care either way.

In Keldarp, that was enough.

CHAPTER 30

Keldarp Breathes

A few days later, the coffee cup was warm in Patrik's hand, the porcelain chipped at the rim. He let his thumb rest against it, feeling the slight imperfection as he stared past the low fence. Everything was as it always was on Majvor's porch

The village didn't offer much to look at — a patchwork of roofs, a sagging clothesline in the neighbor's yard, the faint glint of a tractor moving slow along a distant field. Nothing out of place. Nothing that hinted at what had settled beneath the surface.

The breeze stirred the scent of cut grass and something sweet from Majvor's flowerbeds. He didn't know the names of the plants. Never had. She did, of course. She always did.

His gaze followed a pair of birds flitting between the power lines, their wings sharp against the pale sky. They didn't stay long. Just enough to notice. Just enough to remind him that life moved whether anyone watched or not.

The coffee had cooled by the time he raised it to his lips again. He drank it anyway. Bitter, strong — the way Majvor made it when she knew he wasn't here for conversation.

Beyond the fence, a child's laugh rang out. Brief. Unconcerned. Patrik let his eyes close for a moment, listening to the quiet that followed.

Inside the fence, but apart. That was enough.

The breeze shifted, carrying with it the low hum of a tractor somewhere beyond sight. Steady. Familiar. A sound that belonged here, smoothing over the edges of what had been.

Patrik set the empty cup down on the wooden table beside him. The faint clink of porcelain against wood was swallowed by the distant rhythm of life returning to routine.

A dog barked twice — sharp, then done. A screen door creaked open on a neighboring house, hinges protesting before falling silent again. Footsteps on gravel faded toward the road.

Children's voices drifted through the air, scattered and light. Not the shrill chaos of playgrounds — just fragments. A shout. A laugh. The thud of a ball against a wall.

Somewhere, a radio played. Faint danceband, warped by distance and wind. The kind of music no one really listened to, but always seemed to be on.

Patrik let it all settle around him. The village was good at this — stitching over the gaps, filling them with noise that asked no questions.

The breeze brought the scent of manure next, mingling with cut grass and diesel. He breathed it in without reaction. It was just Keldarp — pretending nothing had happened.

The soft scrape of a chair leg against the porch floor broke the rhythm of distant sounds. Patrik didn't turn. He heard the familiar weight of Majvor's steps — slow, certain.

The coffee pot appeared beside him, its metal surface catching a muted glint of sunlight. No words. Just the gentle tilt of her hand, the quiet pour filling his cup once more.

The smell rose with the steam — bitter, strong, the same as before. It wasn't about taste. It never was.

Majvor sat down without a sigh or a comment, her gaze following his toward the fence and whatever lay beyond it. The breeze played with the edge of the tablecloth, lifting it just enough to show the worn wood beneath.

Patrik wrapped his hands around the cup again, letting the heat settle into his palms. He didn't thank her. She didn't expect it.

A bird landed on the fence post — a flash of wings, then stillness. It watched them with the same quiet they offered in return.

This was life here. A refill of coffee. A view that never changed. No need to speak when everything worth saying had already been understood.

Majvor lifted her cup again, held it halfway to her lips. Then, quietly—

"I hear they never found the mother."

Patrik didn't answer right away. He watched the steam rise, then vanish.

"No."

She set the cup down with care. "And he didn't leave a note? Not even that."

He nodded once. Just confirming what they both already knew.

The breeze stirred again. No birds this time. Just the wind, and what it didn't carry.

The bird was gone when Patrik lifted his eyes. Only the empty fence post remained, weathered and splintered where generations of birds had perched before.

The village stretched beyond, unchanged. A curtain fluttered in a window across the street. A man walked toward the QStar station, a fuel can swinging at his side. Somewhere, a child called out a name, the reply lost to distance.

Majvor sipped her coffee, the faintest clink as her cup met the saucer again. She didn't speak. Neither did he.

The breeze shifted once more — warmer now, carrying the scent of sunlit wood and distant fry oil from Napoli. Life moving forward, not out of hope, but habit.

Patrik let his gaze rest on the village that had already begun to forget. Not out of malice. Just the way things were.

He took another sip, the coffee lukewarm, and set the cup down carefully.

Keldarp didn't need forgiveness or reckoning. It needed routine. The tractors would keep humming, the gossip would soften, and the days would fold into each other until even the sharpest memories dulled. The events wouldn't be forgotten. They would just be hidden. As always. Beneath the lid.

The wind stirred the leaves. A door closed somewhere. The village exhaled — steady, indifferent.

Keldarp breathed again.

REVIEW REQUEST

If you read this far — thank you. And if the story stayed with you, I'd like to ask for a small favor. Please consider leaving a review.

Even a few words of honest feedback can make a real difference.

No need to write much. Just say what stayed with you.

| Amazon Review | Goodreads review |

Thank you — not just for reading, but for sharing your thoughts. That's all this book ever asked for. Scan the QR code to start.

— Ulf Brånebro

FACEBOOK

I'm not a public person, but I keep a quiet presence on Facebook — mostly for readers who want to follow along.

That's where I post early updates about the next books in the *Coffinville* series. Sometimes background details. Sometimes the pieces I had to leave out.

It's also where I hear from readers. If you ever want to ask something, share a thought, or tell me what stayed with you — I read every message. I may not always reply quickly, but I always listen.

No noise. No spam. Just stories, and the people who care about them. Scan the QR code to find me.

—Ulf Brånebro

Printed in Dunstable, United Kingdom